BAD
WEATHER

BAD
WEATHER

A DEZ ROUBIDEAUX
NOVELLA

PAUL
AUSTIN
ARDOIN

ISBN 978-1-949082-05-0
Cover design by Ziad Ezzat
Author photo by Monica Toohey-Krause of Studio KYK
Edited by Max Christian Hansen
Information about the author can be found at
http://www.paulaustinardoin.com

10   9   8   7   6   5   4   3   2   1

TABLE OF CONTENTS

PROLOGUE

THE RAIN POUNDED AGAINST THE FLOOR-TO-CEILING windows of the large, carpeted lobby at the Los Angeles Arts Center. A table stood at one end of the lobby, with a white man in a tweed jacket sitting behind it and a stack of hardback books on top. A line of people stretched from the table all the way across the lobby, past the concession stand, to the corner where the sign for the restrooms shone dimly. A security guard, his arms folded, stood ten feet behind the man.

The man behind the table took a book from the person at the front of the line, signed it, and handed it back; the process then repeated. Sometimes the person in line had more than one book. Sometimes the man would take a book off the stack of hardbacks, sign that, and point to a woman at a smaller table with a placard reading *Cashier*. Often the person in line would talk with the man signing the books. Most of the conversations lasted less than thirty seconds.

Seventy minutes after the start of the signing, two women, one black with short tightly-curled hair, and one Asian with long straight black hair, made it to the front of the line. They were both in their early twenties. The black woman, carrying both a paperback and a hardback in one hand, wore a short black dress, the Asian woman a short dress with a red-and-black floral print.

"You're next," the man said.

"My friend just bought your new book," the black woman said. The Asian woman set down a hardback book in front of him.

"Who should I make it out to?"

"Audrey." With her elbow, the black woman nudged the Asian woman, who crossed her arms and spoke.

"Have him sign your copy of *Exodus Nights* too."

"I don't know—"

"Sorry," Audrey said to the man. "My friend Desirée is apparently embarrassed that she has one of your paperbacks instead of a hardback. But I told her you'd *gladly* sign it."

"Of course," he said.

The woman called Desirée rolled her eyes and set the paperback of *Exodus Nights* down in front of him, next to the hardback.

The man's eyes went to the cover of the other book in her hand. "What the hell is that?" he said softly.

Desirée looked from the cover of the book to the man's face and back again.

"I don't know what you're playing at," the man continued, "but get the hell out of line. And don't *ever* come to one of my events again."

The woman didn't move, staring at the man behind the table. The security guard took two steps forward.

"Sorry," she said. "I didn't realize it would upset you." She turned and put her hand on Audrey's arm. "Come on, let's go."

"What's happening?" Audrey said.

"He saw the other book."

Behind Audrey, another female voice released a bloodcurdling scream.

Desirée pulled Audrey behind her; Audrey caught her heel on the carpet and fell to the floor.

A white woman dressed in black jeans and a black hooded sweatshirt ran screaming into the lobby. She knocked over the display of hardback books, and held out a hunting knife with her right hand.

The man jumped out of his chair, and the woman slashed at him. The blade caught the man's right forearm, cutting through the sleeve of the tweed jacket. A small spray of blood came out as the man stumbled backward.

The white woman in the hooded sweatshirt screamed again, and raised the knife.

The security guard stepped forward.

Three gunshots.

1

Three Months Earlier

FIVE DAYS OF RAIN AND NO SIGNS OF LETTING UP. THE carpet in front of Dez Roubideaux's door had started to get black.

Dez sat on the checkered sofa, trying to ignore the stains in the carpet. Her roommate Rhonda constantly tracked in mud and didn't wipe her feet, and it was also her turn to vacuum the living room this week, a duty she seemed to be ignoring. Dez picked up the remote control from the coffee table. She clicked away from MTV to the Weather Channel and sat back, bleakly staring the big blue capital L on the screen, the low pressure system off the Southern California coast which was sending bad weather to the whole Los Angeles area. The L just sat there, not moving—giving no clues if it would move on in the next couple of days, or if it would stick around another week—maybe even through the end of January.

Dez had hoped to avoid this kind of weather when she joined the criminal justice program at Cal State Long Beach. She was a long way from the bayous of Lake Charles, but somehow it was never quite far enough. She turned the slip of paper over in her hand—*Frankie*. The 310 area code and seven digits were written plainly underneath.

The door swung open hard, and Rhonda, a tall, muscular, olive-skinned woman, came in. Her windbreaker shed water like dandelions expelling white fluff in a stiff breeze. She had her mountain bike up off the ground, hefting it over one shoulder, her backpack, sopping wet, on the other.

"*¿Qué onda?*" Rhonda said. "Really coming down out there." She said it like she was proud of it.

Dez got up to open the sliding glass door so Rhonda could put her bike in their covered, fenced-in patio. She deliberately ignored Rhonda's Adidas squishing through the living room and kitchen before she went out the back door.

Dez went back to the sofa and absentmindedly turned the paper over and over in her hand. Out of the corner of her eye, she saw Rhonda on the patio, shedding the windbreaker and hanging it over the bike before she came in. Rhonda kicked off her shoes. Her eyes lit on the slip of paper in Dez's hand and she smirked.

"Oh, come on, Dez, don't tell me you haven't called her yet."

"What?"

"Don't do this to yourself," Rhonda said. "You already cleaned the kitchen. You reorganized your CDs like five times. Just pick up the phone."

"Now, Rhonda, don't pretend like you got this white girl all figured out," Dez said. "Maybe she's straight."

"She knew all the lyrics to 'Bring Me Some Water,'" Rhonda said. "She's not straight."

"Well then, maybe she's not home."

"Leave a message on her machine. It's not that hard."

"Maybe—"

"Dez, we did *not* drive all the way up to a party in Westwood just so you'd get scared off by some hot pin-up girl wannabe. Pick up the damn phone." Rhonda went up the stairs, clomping in her wet socks, leaving Dez alone with Frankie's number and the Weather Channel.

Dez swore under her breath. She hated when Rhonda was right. She went over to the telephone table and picked up their cordless phone and dialed.

"Hello?"

"Hello," Dez said, her heart racing. "Is Frankie there?"

Dez liked the name Frankie. She liked deliberately taking a very feminine name and masculinizing it. It was what she had done to *Desirée*, after all. And shortening *Francine* or *Francesca* certainly qualified—plus, there were so many interesting connotations. *Frankie and Johnnie*, with the old song's passion and heartbreak. *Frankie Goes To Hollywood*, the mention of which took Dez back a couple of years, hearing "Relax" at the all-ages club in Long Beach, before a white girl in dark red lipstick, who acted like she owned the place, started calling her names. And "Relax" made her think of sneaking into see *Body Double* at the movie theater back in Lake Charles, and seeing Melanie Griffith naked—well, that was right about the time Dez realized she was different from other girls.

Dez also liked that the nickname contained the word *frank*, which *Francine* and *Franscesca* didn't have. Frankness, openness, honesty. Which she could use more of in her life. Dez had gone through a breakup a couple of years before with Connie—whose name invoked just the opposite qualities: con man, con job, pros and cons.

At the party in Westwood, Dez didn't think Frankie looked like a Frankie. She looked like she had been a tomboy growing up, the kind of girl who wore flannel men's shirts in high school but every boy still had a crush on. At the party, she wore a dress—one of the few girls there *in* a dress—and turned many heads. The dress, a summery, almost 1950's pin-up style dress, had red cherries and green stems and leaves on a white background. The dress straps tied around her neck, and her curves pulled off the pin-up look without going overboard on the hair and makeup.

She had come up to Dez—one of the few black girls at the party—and when she introduced herself, Dez didn't think *Frankie* on any level. She thought *Lauren*, or maybe *Elizabeth*, but nothing that ended in an "ee" sound—it didn't go with the dress. Dez saw where her dress strap met her collarbone and just stood there as she offered her hand. Dez finally took it, and looked up—looked at her large eyes, her wide mouth, her porcelain skin, too surreal to touch. But her hand was strong, her grip firm, her skin cool.

"This is Frankie," the voice at the other end of the phone said.

Dez started, shaking herself out of her reverie. "Hey, Frankie, this is Dez. I went to that party last Friday. Over in Westwood."

"Oh, Dez, hi!" she said. "I danced with you to 'Tainted Love.'"

"Yep, that's me all right," Dez said. She wanted to ask Frankie her last name, but couldn't think of how to do it. And suddenly, Dez realized that she had been psyching herself up for so long about picking up the phone and calling Frankie that she hadn't actually thought of anything to say to her.

"You want to go to dinner on Friday?" Dez blurted out. She hadn't meant to say it, especially this early in the conversation; she wanted to appear cool. But she had said it, thrust out there now. All she could do was wait.

There was a pause, during which Dez could only hear the blood pounding in her ears. "I'm meeting my agent on Friday night in Hollywood," Frankie said. "It's a whole production, he wants me to meet with some people. But if you're free tonight, I could go for some coffee or dessert."

Dez heard the word *agent* and was thrown off a little. "No problem," Dez said. "I can do that." She had a class at nine the next morning—and she had promised herself that she'd stop going on dates the night before an early class. But she remembered Frankie, and that pin-up dress, and thought she could make an exception.

"Where did you say you were?" Frankie said. "You're near Huntington Beach or something, right?"

"Oh, no. I'm not *that* far. I'm just a few miles down the road. In Long Beach."

"And I'm in Redondo Beach," Frankie said. "So many beaches." She laughed. It was a bad joke—not really a joke at all. It was a genuine laugh, though; Frankie seemed comfortable in her own skin, and Dez was immediately envious.

Dez realized there was a pause in the conversation and started to panic about what to say. She grasped at the first thing she remembered.

"Now did I hear that right? You say you're meeting your agent?"

"Right," Frankie said.

"What do you have an agent for?" As soon as she heard the words leave her mouth, Dez winced. That didn't come out the way she wanted it to.

Frankie clicked her tongue. "I thought for sure Linda would have told you."

"Nope, she didn't say anything to me." Dez had no idea who Linda was. Maybe she lived at the party house in Westwood.

"I'm a writer."

"Oh, cool," Dez said, not recognizing the tone in her voice. "What kind of stuff do you write?"

"Novels, mostly," Frankie said offhandedly. "I have a book of short stories that didn't sell very well and a memoir my agent didn't want to touch."

"Novels," Dez said. She liked crime novels and mysteries, although with each criminal justice class she took, her enjoyment of the books dampened; she was starting to see that the way things worked in the novels was a fantasy compared to how the police actually investigated. She had found herself, lately, reading P.D. James and Martha Grimes: British writers using the unfamiliar Scotland Yard as a backdrop didn't mess with her sense of reality quite as much. And, upon the advice of a couple of her friends, she had read some Toni Morrison and Patricia Cornwall the last year, although she found them more depressing than empowering.

"I guess you'd call it 'literary fiction,'" Frankie said, then stifled a yawn. "I just write the stories as the muse dictates, of course, but I find genre fiction—and especially romance and police procedurals—all so tiresome."

Dez winced. She'd never read a Harlequin romance—they weren't written for her—but she'd cut her teeth on Ed McBain.

"And I'd like to wring Stephen King's neck," Frankie continued. "Now everybody thinks they can put a rabid dog or a murderous clown into a story and be the next big thing."

"Well, I hate to say this, but I don't think I've heard of you—what's your last name?" Dez asked. She tapped her pencil eraser on the table a few times in succession.

"Oh, I don't use my real last name on my literary fiction." Frankie's tone was distracted, buoyant. Dez felt like the conversation was a helium balloon and she was desperately trying to hang onto the string.

"Really? I thought for sure that most people would *want* their name on literary novels. You don't want to leave your fake names for the crappy formula novels that put food on the table?"

Frankie cleared her throat. "I guess I'm not most people."

Dez nodded. She could feel her throat go dry. "So, uh, what name do you use?"

"Oh, right. I use my middle name as my last name."

There was silence for a moment. "And what's your middle name?" Dez finally asked.

"Bethany."

"Oh, wow, Bethany. Now that's a beautiful name." The words were out of Dez's mouth before she could stop them, and she silently cursed herself. The string of the conversation balloon slipped through her fingers.

"Thank you, I guess."

No use stopping now, Dez thought. "Hey, I'm not joking, girl. I really like that name."

"Fine."

"Frankie Bethany, novelist. I like the sound of that." Dez started to walk around the coffee table, holding the portable phone tightly to her ear. She actually wasn't sure if she liked the sound of the name, but it was too late—and too pointless—to back out of it now. The two double-e sounds at the end of each name sounded too playful. It wasn't sober enough for a serious novelist. Perhaps that was why Dez had never heard of her writing before.

"So," Dez said. "You said you were free for coffee tonight?"

"Sure. There's a cool little bistro just a few blocks away from me. They're open late, and they make some nice after-dinner coffee drinks. Or if you're feeling adventurous, I think they have some limoncello."

Dez had never had limoncello, but she had heard Rhonda talk about getting the worst hangover in the world from it. "Yeah, that sounds good."

Frankie gave Dez directions to her apartment. "When did we say? Eight?"

"Eight sounds great," Dez said. "See you then, *chica*."

Dez hung up, her heart still pounding in her ears. Had she really called Frankie *chica*? She backtracked around the coffee table as if the phone hadn't been cordless and she had to unwrap herself. She put the phone back on the cradle to charge.

"Sounds like someone's got a hot date," Rhonda called from upstairs.

"Aw, shit, Rhonda, you were listening?"

Rhonda's head appeared at the top of the stairs. "Of course I was listening." She started to walk down and stopped about halfway, sitting on a step. "Nothing exciting ever happens here. You're going to be the most boring cop in the world if you keep this up. But now you're going on a date with a hotshot *artiste*. Maybe you can be her kept woman and just sit around eating bonbons all day."

Dez laughed, a little uneasily. "I don't know about that. She's written books. I don't think she's rich."

"Don't play me, girl. I know a sugar mama when I see one. She's gotta be older than you, Dez. You were talking about agents and shit?"

"Yeah, I guess."

Rhonda got a thoughtful look on her face. "She sure doesn't *look* older than you, though. I saw you watching her at the party. Incredible body. All boobs and butt. I could do with one of those girls."

"Get your own *artiste*."

"Hey, I'm on your side on this one, Dez. She's hot. I like the artistic thing. I bet she's a little crazy."

"Okay, whatever."

"I mean crazy in bed."

"Yeah, Rhonda, I got that. You don't ever mean another kind of crazy."

Rhonda grinned, a wicked smile that spread slowly across her face, as she stretched her arms above her head. "All right, I've got an early class tomorrow, and I've got a paper that isn't going to write itself. You have fun with your little poetess."

"Author."

"Whatever. Tell me all the juicy details when you get home. Let me know if you're moving in with her."

"Shut up, Rhonda."

"Seriously. I need a new roommate. Maybe someone with a decent toaster oven." Rhonda flashed an evil smile at Dez and cackled, pulling herself to her feet and walking back upstairs.

Dez watched Rhonda disappear, and looked at the clock on the wall. It was only five-forty-five.

She walked around the house for a few minutes. The rain was still coming down, and it was the kind of rain she was tired of. She noticed a dirty spot on the sofa cushion where Rhonda must have put her feet up.

Dez turned on the television. It was still on the Weather Channel. The topic hadn't changed, either: the big blue L, down from the Gulf of Alaska, wasn't giving Los Angeles a break from the rain anytime soon.

Dez could feel herself getting restless. Now that there was a countdown before she had to pick Frankie up, she was distracted. She pointed the remote at the television, flipping around the stations, but nothing held her interest.

Finally, after about ten minutes, she turned off the television and grabbed her car keys. She could use some dinner. And maybe she should do some research on her date, as well.

She went to the hall closet and took out her rain jacket; light, but fleece-lined, and with a hood. It glistened, still wet from the rain earlier in the afternoon. Though the boxy design didn't especially flatter her figure, Dez thought it went well with the tight-jeans-and-Oxford-shirt aesthetic she had perfected—which, she hoped, had attracted Frankie. She had warmer jackets; the Union Bay blue-checked polarfleece one came to mind, as it was cold—at least by Southern California standards—but the polarfleece didn't stand up well to heavy rain. She spent a couple of minutes looking in vain for an umbrella and decided the hood would do.

Dez looked out the window. The sky had grown darker, the rain a little heavier. It was the kind of wet that got into everything, soaking Dez's Levi's, getting through to her socks, and leaving her shoes squishing around for several days. Dez sighed. She knew her car was damp inside from the rain tracked into it, and it wouldn't be the most impressive vehicle to take an inspired writer like Frankie in. Frankie, who had an agent. The agent probably wined and dined Frankie in a fancy European car with leather seats before proffering the contract with the big advance.

Dez ran her hand over her short, tightly curled hair. Her hair had mostly dried out after the rainstorm that afternoon, and she wasn't looking forward to getting it soaked again—especially not when she was trying to impress somebody. She hoped the hood would be effective enough.

She didn't want to drive all the way to Redondo Beach; she didn't even want to wade through the rain in the parking lot to get to her car. But she did really want to see Frankie.

She picked up her purse and opened the door to the pouring rain.

2

THE BOOKSTORE WAS CROWDED, AND AT THE ENTRANCE people jostled each other to get in out of the rain, and made almost no eye contact. Perhaps the darkened sky made them feel introspective and moody.

She had chosen BookEarth off Artesia Boulevard, more or less on the way to Redondo Beach. She'd heard about the huge selection, and it truly was a massive book store. But she wasn't too familiar with the layout. She stepped around the New Releases tables—mostly big stacks of hardback editions of *Needful Things* and *The Sum of All Fears*, although a few copies of Alison Weir's *The Six Wives of Henry VIII* were placed in a small stack on one of the back tables.

It took her a moment to find the *Fiction & Literature* section. She went on a search for Frankie Bethany in the "A–B" bookcase. A bearded man with thick, black plastic rimmed glasses and a brown fedora was reading Jean M. Auel's *The Clan of the Cave Bear*. He glanced at Dez and took a small step to the side.

She looked at the shelves near the bottom. There was a thin but noticeable layer of dust in front of the books: John Barth, Samuel Beckett, Saul Bellow, and then at the end of the shelf, she saw it.

"Bethany," read the thick spine. "Exodus Nights." Then in smaller print, with a modern art-deco logo: "Showcase Monument Contemporaries." There were two copies of *Exodus Nights* on the shelf, right next to each other. She picked up the one on the end. The books were so thick that the second copy didn't budge when its twin was removed, even with the weight of the other books against it.

She flipped to the end of the book. 678 pages, and the type was fairly small. It was a massive tome, but that didn't scare off Dez; she was used to thousand-page Stephen King books that Frankie apparently despised. She tried not to look at any of the words on the last page as she closed the book and flipped it over to look at the cover.

The cover was dark, predominantly black: a photograph of a man in a suit, his back to the camera, running into a stylized field of dark blue that blended smoothly into the blackness of the rest of the cover. "Exodus Nights" was below the photograph, and at the top, in larger text than the title, were the words "Frank Bethany."

Hm, Dez thought. *That's interesting.*

Dez turned the book back over and began to read the reviews.

The critical acclaim impressed her. "Nominated for the PEN/Faulkner Award." "An astonishing debut, rich in texture and character." "Bethany's language is brilliant...the ambitious scope of the plot is matched by the assuredness of the writer." "Bethany writes with such clarity that it's hard to escape the emotional heft of many scenes." "A stunning work." "A tour de force."

"Well, now *that* must be worth reading," Dez murmured.

The bearded man looked up. "You talking about *Exodus Nights*?"

Dez glanced behind her and then realized he was talking to her. "Oh. Uh-huh. It looks pretty good."

"It's a real page-turner," the man said. "It's really powerful, too. It's not one of those beachy summer reads that you don't really have to pay attention to. I totally lost myself in it. It's long, but I probably finished it in a couple of days." He laughed. "I think I even called in sick to work just so I could read it."

"This is Bethany's debut novel?"

"Yeah, he's got a couple of other ones too. *Friendly Fire*, I think the second one is called. It's good, but it's nowhere near as good as *Exodus Nights*."

Dez wondered if she had missed something in the conversation with Frankie. Did Dez even have the right author? "Now, this is a local author, right?" Dez ventured.

The man shook his head, reached into the book as Dez was holding it, and turned to the end section, behind the last page. There was a poorly-reproduced black-and-white photo of a white man, with a mop of medium-toned hair, wearing a leather jacket. There was a short biography of Frank Bethany, from the minor literary awards he'd won with his short fiction to the announcement of his fourth book scheduled for publication the following spring. The bio ended with, "Bethany lives in New Hampshire with his wife and two Rottweilers."

Dez's head spun a bit. Was this an elaborate ruse to disguise Frankie's gender? Was there something in the book that didn't connect with a female author writing it? Or was Frankie lying? Dez wasn't sure why Frankie would lie to her, though, especially over something so easily provable.

She carried the book with her to the information desk, and the young Asian woman with glasses behind the desk looked at Dez expectantly. Dez thought the woman was stunning, and had to stammer to get the words out. "I'm looking for novelists with the last name *Bethany*," she said. "I found Frank Bethany—obviously—but I was looking for a female writer."

The woman nodded. "Any idea at all on the first name?"

Dez shook her head. The woman's eyes, even hidden by the glasses, were breathtaking—so much so that she almost forgot about Frankie. She glanced at the woman's nametag: *Audrey*.

"There's a co-author of a book on the writings of Jacques Derrida named Marie Bethany-François," Audrey said. "I could special order that—oh, that's a textbook. It's quite expensive."

Dez shook her head. "No, no problem. I must have heard the name wrong or something."

The woman nodded. "Perhaps it's the woman's first name. We have dozens of listings for novelists with the first name of Bethany."

Dez shook her head. "No, that's not going to be it. But thanks anyway," Dez said.

She walked to the counter and stood in line. The bearded man was a few people in front of her, buying a small stack of four books. Dez couldn't tell if *The Clan of the Cave Bear* was in there.

The line seemed to take a long time to get through. Dez checked her watch; she still had almost two hours to eat some dinner and drive the remaining twelve or so miles to Frankie's apartment. The bearded man bought his books; he caught Dez's eye and nodded, smiling. Dez nodded back, feeling phony. She got to the front of the line and pulled a ten-dollar bill out of her wallet. The teenager behind the second register motioned her over. He looked at the book and then at her.

"This is really good," he said. "Very intense, but really good."

Dez had an urge to tell him that she knew the author, but kept her mouth shut. "Yeah, you know, that's what I heard," she responded instead. "I heard it was better than his other ones too."

The clerk leaned forward conspiratorially. "I liked *Friendly Fire* better," he whispered. "I like it because it's not as graphic, which I guess makes me a fag or something, but whatever. Better characters, too."

Dez blinked hard at the clerk's casual use of the pejorative term, and she wondered if she'd ever get used to it—movies, television, people on the street. She forced herself to smile.

"That'll be nine seventy-three," he said, putting the book in a plastic bag.

Dez handed over the ten and he gave her a quarter and two pennies.

"Enjoy your book," he said. "Keep it dry."

Dez, tight-lipped, simply nodded.

There was a Burger King farther along the parking lot and she went there to get something cheap to eat. The bistro's drinks might be expensive—in her experience, calling a restaurant a *bistro* was just a license to charge fifty percent more and treat the customers badly.

She made sure the book was protected by the plastic bag and walked quickly across the parking lot to the Burger King. She pulled the door open and went in. The tile floor, which looked suspiciously like outdoor tile, had wet shoe prints all over the area in front of the door. Like weakening waves emanating from a rock dropped in the middle of a pool, the shoe prints got lighter and more spread out the farther away from the door it was.

There was no one in line and only a few people eating at the tables. Dez ordered, took her Coke, sat at one of the tables, and took out *Exodus Nights*.

The first page had Dez hooked.

The book opened with a detached account of a murder on a lifeboat at twilight. The victim was a man, that much was plain, but his relationship to the other people on the lifeboat was obfuscated. It also was unclear who the killer was—there were six people on the lifeboat, and there was a hunting knife the man had used to gut a fish several hours earlier. But the text, while passionate and lurid, took no pains to identify the one who actually stabbed the man.

It was clear, however, that everyone on the lifeboat wanted him dead. Everyone, that is, except for one man. He was elderly, had clear mental problems, and didn't seem to understand, much less judge, what the other people did.

Dez heard her number called and got her food, bringing it back to the table. She unwrapped part of her burger so she could it eat it with one hand and went back to the book.

After the victim's body was thrown overboard and the sky went dark, the remaining people on the boat fell into an uneasy sleep. They were awakened by the sound of a Navy helicopter at sunrise.

The narrator followed the elderly man to the hospital, which was quite surreal. Dez wasn't sure of the location or the year, which she suspected was the author's intent; still, it was off-putting, especially as a parade of hospital staff and visitors, each increasingly bizarre, visited the old man, poked and prodded him, asked personal and inappropriate questions, and left.

The last visitors were a male doctor and a female nurse, who callously grilled the old man about his sex life, but they were details from long ago, from a wife long passed away, and then the doctor and nurse began to kiss, began to undress each other, and then transformed before his eyes into wolves, who then started to copulate, transforming again into large, Kafkaesque insects, also copulating, finally transforming back into people, but the doctor was now a woman with similar facial features to the male doctor; vice versa for the male nurse. The doctor and nurse finished coupling—described rather graphically, but clinically—and proclaimed the old man healed. The old man was grateful, tears running down his face.

Dez realized she had been holding her breath, and breathed in and out deliberately. And stopped to think.

The weird, off-putting scene still made Dez marvel at the smooth, clear prose. Most writers wouldn't be able to write that kind of scene without completely confusing the reader. Yes, the actual happenings were bizarre—*beyond* bizarre—but the straightforward writing style gave no opening for ambiguity, even as the wolves transformed into insects. Even in the clarity, the occasional clever metaphor gave perfect if disturbing mental pictures; vivid descriptions of the doctor and nurse, the two wolves, the two insects, the transformed doctor and nurse felt complete instead of drawn-out. None of it felt forced, none of it was over the top—crazy, given the over-the-top potential of the scene.

Dez looked at her watch: a quarter to eight. She cursed quietly; she had been reading so long that she was going to be late. She hoped that traffic wouldn't be too bad, but knew that she'd be at least ten minutes late.

Dez's head swam with the onslaught of lifeboats and characters and wolves and insects and grisly murders. Distracted, she crossed the parking lot, forgetting to pull her hood up, and got in the car. She smiled. Thoughts of Frankie stopped her from obsessing about the bad weather. That was probably a good thing.

She drove down Artesia Boulevard, and miraculously hit most of the green lights. But her luck ran out when she made a left on Hawthorne, and it crawled for a couple of miles until she finally escaped onto Sepulveda.

At a red light, she looked at the address again, and realized that Frankie's address wasn't in Redondo Beach; it was across the city limit in Torrance, although not by much. Dez grunted. She didn't like it when people put on airs. On the other hand, she reasoned, it was closer to her apartment than going all the way down to the PCH or to Esplanade. And it was so much easier to forgive Frankie since she was attractive and interesting.

She missed the apartment complex at first, and had to make a U-turn. She found a spot marked VISITOR and checked her watch. She was seven minutes late, which was pretty good considering the backup on Hawthorne. She looked at herself in the mirror of her visor. Her hair had started to frizz. She kept it short for manageability, plus her first girlfriend had liked it short, and it had shocked her mother. The rain had slowed to a drizzle, and Dez took off her boxy rain jacket and left it in the car.

She had no idea where Apartment 16 would be, but she quickly found it; it was a ground-floor apartment on the end. She rang the doorbell and waited. And waited.

She checked her watch; it was ten minutes past. Scenarios ran through her head. Frankie *had* said tonight, right? What exactly had Frankie said over the phone? No—Frankie had definitely said tonight. She leaned over and rang the doorbell again.

She strained to listen for signs of life inside. The lights were on, but she could hear neither a television nor stereo. She knocked, feeling silly. Still nothing.

She was about to walk away when Frankie opened the door.

3

THE RED-AND-WHITE CHERRY DRESS WAS GONE, THE
1950s pin-up look replaced by thin-rimmed glasses, a
tight aquamarine pullover sweater, and black palazzo
pants. Frankie's long brown hair was pulled back in a
simple French braid. If the pin-up look had piqued Dez's
interest, this presentation—bordering on "hot librar-
ian"—made her pulse race.

"I bet it's eight o'clock already," Frankie said, stepping aside to let Dez in.

The front door opened into a small living room, with
a kitchen and dining nook directly beyond. The place
smelled of computer paper. The living room, neither
immaculate nor messy, was filled with furniture: in
roughly the center, a sofa with a brown-and-gold rose
pattern at least fifteen years out of date, that nonethe-
less looked well cared for. In front of this, a coffee table,

on which were two stacks of paper, and between them an empty box of Chinese food with two cheap wooden chopsticks sticking out. Behind the sofa, a computer desk with an IBM PS/2, a monochrome monitor blaring its blue-and-white beacons, a keyboard and mouse drawer, and a printer below. Next to the wall facing the sofa, a small TV stand with a nineteen-inch television. The television was pushed back on the cart just enough to leave a ledge for the nearly-empty wineglass that stood there, blocking the screen.

The rabbit ears of the television were extended fully and at crazy angles, making Dez think Frankie wasn't a fan of cable. The wineglass blocking the view of the screen made Dez think maybe Frankie wasn't a fan of television at all.

A small stack of paperbacks perched on top of the computer monitor, and against the wall next to the television, two large bookcases almost reached the ceiling, stuffed with books. The bottom shelf contained mostly reference books—a Merriam-Webster dictionary, a Spanish/English dictionary, and other hardbound tomes, then a sea of color in the spines swooped up to the top shelf. Frankie had more books than bookshelf space, and she had placed some titles horizontally, over the top of the vertically placed books. Dez wanted to take a closer look but didn't want to seem nosy.

"Well, I'm ten minutes late," Dez said, smirking, as Frankie closed the door, "but you know it's all your fault." She took a couple of steps toward the bookshelf. Paul Bowles' *The Sheltering Sky* was in there. She also saw the familiar art-deco spine of Toni Morrison's *Beloved* and the near match of *Tar Baby*, but on different shelves, making Dez cringe at the thought of Frankie not arranging her books in alphabetical order by author last name. *Maybe she just put her books in randomly* was Dez's next thought, and was unsurprised that it gave her almost as much stress as reading *Exodus Nights*.

Frankie made a clicking noise with her tongue, the same sound Dez had heard on the phone earlier. "My fault?" Dez looked at Frankie's expressionless face; she obviously hadn't caught Dez's smirk.

"Yep," Dez said, trying to sound a lot more confident than she felt. "I went out and bought *Exodus Nights* before dinner, and I got all caught up in it. Lost track of time."

"Ah," Frankie responded, a smile touching the corners of her mouth.

Dez's heart raced. Had she revealed too much too soon? Was the fact that she bought the book right away going to look desperate? Overly interested? Stalker-ish? After all, Rebecca Shaeffer, the actress who had been shot point-blank by an obsessed fan just three years earlier, had lived just a few miles away.

Frankie was stooping over the coffee table to pick up the Chinese food carton when she said, "So, um, I guess you've got a few questions for me." She turned her back on Dez and walked to the kitchen, where, to judge by the sound, she put the carton in the trash.

When she emerged a moment later, Dez shrugged, trying to pretend she wasn't burning with curiosity. "I think the Frank Bethany pseudonym is pretty clever."

"You think so, huh?"

"Of course I do." Dez paused, wondering how much more she should say. She decided to push one more time. "Nice picture, too, although I'd have to say the likeness isn't very good. I hate to say it, but the camera makes you look decades older."

Frankie smiled. "And male."

Dez put her hands up in a mock gesture. "Hey, I'm not here to judge."

Frankie laughed. Her teeth were white and straight. Even without the cherry dress, she had a pinup type of beauty in her face. Large eyes, high cheekbones, a round face.

Dez caught herself staring, then cleared her throat. "Well, if I'm taking you to coffee tonight—"

"And *dessert*, Dez. Don't sell me short."

Dez smiled, though she hadn't remembered a mention of dessert on the phone. Limoncello, yes, but not dessert. "Coffee *and* dessert, sure. But you think I oughta get to know a little bit more about you?"

"Like what?" Frankie said, going to the hall closet and pulling out a jacket on a hanger. "Is it still raining out there?"

"Just a drizzle," Dez said. "And like maybe your real name?"

Frankie laughed, putting the jacket back. "You don't think *Frank Bethany* is good enough?"

"If I were your editor, sure enough," Dez said. "But I'm not your editor, I'm your date."

"You sure sound like my editor, trying to convince me to put Exodus Nights out under a man's name."

"And that reminds me," said Dez, "who is that guy in your author photo?"

Frankie blinked and hesitated. "That's my Uncle Alex." She started talking faster, like floodgates were opening. "My agent insisted on it. I had to fly Uncle Alex out here from Vermont on my own dime. I was the one who had to get him to their photography studio and everything. I had to hire someone to do his makeup, get his hair right, select his clothes." She folded her arms. "Seriously, you would not *believe* some of the things my agent has me doing for this gender reversal. I thought George Eliot and George Sand sacrificed themselves to make it easier on future generations."

Dez shook her head. "I don't know," she began. "Even ten years ago, women were pretending to be men. You know Dell Shannon?" That was the name mystery writer Elizabeth Linington wrote under. Dez had found Dell Shannon's books in the Lake Charles library, and she had almost burst with excitement to read an American police-procedural author—until then her mystery sustenance had been mostly Hercule Poirot and Inspector Morse. But the thinly-veiled racism in Linington's books had been crushing.

Frankie waved her hand dismissively. "Oh, you don't have to tell me. I know the war hasn't been won yet."

Dez's brain pinballed from Dell Shannon to the campus police officer who detained her outside class for an hour because she looked *suspicious*. But this was Frankie's story, not Dez's, and so she put on her sympathetic face. "It must be hell, for sure, girl."

"Sure is."

"Those Rottweilers were a cute little detail."

"The what?"

"The Rottweilers. You know, 'Frank Bethany lives in New Hampshire with his wife and two Rottweilers.'"

Frankie laughed. "Oh, that's right. I forgot about that. The Rottweilers were my agent's idea."

"And you're not married or anything, either, right?"

Frankie smiled and shook her head.

Dez stood there for a moment, trying to take it all in: the sofa, the kitchen, the bookshelves, the piles of books and papers. Frankie didn't apologize for the state of her apartment; in fact, it hadn't even occurred to her that she should. Dez's mother, after cleaning all day for company, would then greet her visitors with an apology for the nonexistent mess. Maybe Frankie had the right idea.

"So, are you ready to go?" Dez finally said.

Frankie picked up her purse from the kitchen counter. "Sure."

They stepped out into the night, and Frankie locked the door behind them. The rain had finally stopped, and it was cool, but not cold. "What do you think?" Frankie said. "Should we chance a walk to the bistro?"

"I guess it depends how far away it is," Dez said.

"It's just a couple of blocks."

"I can do a couple of blocks."

"Great." Frankie smiled warmly at Dez.

Dez was glad she had left the jacket in the car. With her long-sleeve shirt and dark blue jeans on, she was warm as she walked, and she was hoping she wouldn't break into a sweat. She was glad Frankie had left her jacket at home, too; the aquamarine sweater looked amazing on her. She tried to think of something to say that wasn't about *Exodus Nights*.

"So what are you working on now?" Dez asked, stepping over a puddle.

"I've got outlines for three different books right now." Frankie shrugged. "None of them are particularly appealing to me, though. Everyone wants a sequel to *Exodus Nights*. That's still his biggest seller, you know."

"His? You talking about yourself in the third person?"

Frankie stammered. "Well, sometimes it's hard for me to think that *I'm* actually the one writing that. Since I don't see my actual name on the book cover and all."

The next puddle took up Dez's half of the sidewalk, so she walked behind Frankie. "Is that weird for you? Not seeing your name as an award finalist even though you're the one who wrote everything?"

Frankie shrugged. "I don't know. It would probably seem just as surreal to see *Francesca Bethany* there. And my editor did say that I'd be taken a lot more seriously with all the violence and sex I have in my books if all the readers thought it was a man that wrote it. Maybe I wouldn't have won that award if I wrote under my own name."

"The PEN/Faulkner? I thought the book cover just said you were nominated."

Frankie shrugged again and hesitated. "My agent said the nomination had the same kind of sales bump as a win. Everyone who cares buys all the nominated books anyway."

"So it kind of *is* an honor just to be nominated," Dez joked.

"I guess." Frankie's gaze was in the distance again.

It had only been ten minutes, but the date wasn't going particularly well, Even though Dez was really interested in *Exodus Nights* and why Frankie wrote under a man's name, she racked her brain trying to come up with other things to talk about.

"So who invited you to the party last Friday?" Dez said.

"I came with Bianca."

"Bianca?"

Frankie chuckled. "I don't know her last name either. We were smoking pot over at her house on Wednesday night and she invited us all."

Dez nodded. The conversation had run out of steam again. She figured it was as good a time as any to try to get Frankie's romantic history, even if Dez couldn't get her last name.

"So," Dez said, as casually as she could, "what was the name of your last girlfriend?"

"John," Frankie said.

Dez looked at Frankie and saw that she wasn't kidding. "So you were dating a man last?"

"Well, the last person I was in a relationship with."

"But, you know, you've *been* with girls."

"Oh, yeah," Frankie said, nodding. "I've definitely been with girls."

"Okay," Dez said. "Sorry for the third degree. I've been on a couple of dates with freshman girls who *said* they were bi, but really they just wanted to make their ex-boyfriends jealous."

Frankie laughed, although Dez didn't think it was very funny. "The shit women do for gender expectations, right?"

Dez looked at Frankie, not quite getting where she was going.

"I mean, look at me. I write that lifeboat scene, I write that wolf and insect sex scene in the hospital, and everyone's all like, 'Hey, you can only sell that if you're a *man.*'"

Dez was quiet for a moment.

"And, if that weren't insulting enough, it winds up nominated for all kinds of awards and winds up on a bestseller list and actually proves the publisher *right.*"

"You telling me you couldn't just do an 'F.B. Bethany' and leave it at that?" Dez was halfway hoping Frankie would correct her on the last name, but Frankie didn't take the bait.

Frankie shook her head. "Don't remind me of the fights I had with my editor over that."

They crossed Sepulveda and it became Camino Real and with that change entered the Redondo Beach city limits. Dez thought maybe two blocks away from Redondo Beach was close enough to count, but she still couldn't get a decent handle on Frankie.

"Which way?" Dez asked. Frankie pointed down Camino Real, vaguely enough that Dez still didn't have a good idea where they were going.

"So, is this bistro known for their desserts?" Dez said. She was still curious about Frankie's experiences with the publishers—she had really enjoyed her women's studies class—but she was feeling a rant coming on, and was hoping to make out with Frankie later. A rant might preemptively destroy the possibility of that before it started.

"They should be," Frankie said. "It kind of sucks that they have the best desserts south of San Francisco, and yet they're nowhere near making the best dessert lists."

"Yeah, that's kind of a travesty," Dez said.

Frankie opened her mouth and then closed it. Dez thought maybe she was going to tie the travesty of the bistro not getting recognized to the travesty of her having to write under a man's name to have any success. Dez looked at Frankie and smiled. She was glad there was some semblance of self-control under there.

"So, um, what did you do before you were a writer?" Dez said, ducking under a low-hanging branch. She brushed against it and it showered her with droplets.

"Well, I've always been a writer," Frankie said. "I just didn't get paid for it for the first twenty-five years."

Frankie's too-precious answer annoyed Dez. Frankie's beauty had distracted Dez from taking umbrage at some of her responses, and Dez found much of what Frankie said fascinating. But other times, she seemed like she needed heavy sedation not to go off the rails. Attractive yet maddening: the two weren't mutually exclusive.

Frankie sighed, and it dawned on Dez that she wasn't hiding her annoyance from Frankie particularly well. "I waitressed, mostly," Frankie continued. "I had a job at a barbecue place over in Carson. It wasn't a fancy restaurant, but they charged fancy restaurant prices for good barbecue. Sometimes I made two hundred bucks a night in tips."

"Hey, I waitress too. The money ain't bad when the crowds are decent. Frank Bethany makes more than that for you?"

"Yep," Frankie said. "My agent was right—getting nominated for the Pulitzer was a good as a win."

Dez hesitated. *Exodus Nights* had been nominated for the PEN/Faulkner, not the Pulitzer. Was Frankie really that out of touch with her own work? Or did she really not care about the awards? Or—and Dez realized, the most likely scenario—Frankie purposely misidentified the award so to convey the idea that she didn't care about winning awards.

Ugh, Dez thought. It was the worst kind of phony behavior: pretending not to care.

They came to a light with a red *Don't Walk* signal. Dez looked over at Frankie. The woman did know how to put herself together. The silence stretched out, and Dez scrambled for something to say; it would be an excruciating evening with Frankie if the conversation kept stopping.

Dez was still interested in how she came to write as a man, and she wasn't sure what else they had to talk about. Frankie hadn't asked any information about Dez yet, although perhaps that would come over dessert.

"So how did your agent convince you to change sexes with your author name?" Dez said, not really caring that she was opening the door for an epic rant. "I mean, especially today. Four hundred years ago, sure, I get that it wasn't ladylike, but today?"

"Yes, Dez," Frankie said, "*especially* today." She cleared her throat. "I mean, yes, women had far fewer freedoms four hundred years ago. But the expectations placed on women today are deeply ingrained. The price a woman pays for breaking a gender expectation is probably worse today than it was in the time of Jane Austen."

"Hah," Dez said. "Sounds like you've done a little bit of research on that."

"Only my master's thesis," Frankie said. "Except Frank Bethany made it big before I finished it.."

"So what price does the woman pay today?"

"Well, you read *Exodus Nights*."

"Just the opening chapters." Dez stepped around another puddle.

"Okay, so look at what happens. There's a murder at sea, and it's grislier than just about everything I've read that didn't have *Chainsaw Massacre* in the title."

"Yeah, all right, I'll give you that it was pretty grisly. But you know, I don't think it was *gratuitous* or anything. I mean, it was real clinical. You can't say that about the chainsaw massacre stuff. All of that's *totally gratuitous*."

"Well, thanks, I guess, but look at the other stuff. There's the wolves copulating. And then they transform into insects, and they're still copulating, and then they transform back into people, and they're still copulating."

"Sure, that's a whole lot of copulating. But again, it wasn't like a *Penthouse Forum* letter or anything. *Dear Wolves-and-Insect Copulation Monthly, I never thought this could happen to me, but...*"

"Oh, come on, Dez, be serious."

Dez looked at Frankie, and it was clear from her face that she didn't think Dez's attempt at levity was funny. "Okay," she said. "My bad. Sorry. You mean that women can't sell their stuff if they write that kind of subject matter?"

"Exactly." A shopping center appeared on their left, and the bistro looked to be on the end. "Women aren't supposed to write scenes like that. And certainly not in the kind of grisly, psychotic detail I did." She scoffed. "We're not even supposed to *have* thoughts like that. We're supposed to be *good girls*."

"You don't have to tell *me* what people want me to be like. I've been a dyke for a while now." They started walking across the parking lot, Dez walking carefully around the puddles, Frankie walking through them, not caring about her shoes or the hem of her palazzo pants.

Frankie kept talking, like Dez hadn't even said anything. "Listen—when you know a novel is going to be all violent and sexual and sadistic, but you find out the author is a woman, what do you do?"

"Depends on what bookstore I'm in," Dez said, then thought of Dell Shannon. "Actually, I'd probably buy it. Might be something I'd really like."

"Okay—well, most people would put the book back. Or, actually, most people wouldn't even pick up the book to begin with."

"You serious?"

"Yes, I'm serious," Frankie said, opening the bistro door. Dez followed her in. "They'd walk over to another section. Stephen King, Bret Easton Ellis, Tom Wolfe— they can all write about these violent, sexual topics. Women have to write about love and heaving bosoms. Or thin allegorical feminist manifestos masquerading as fiction." They stood at the hostess stand, in front of the *Please Wait to Be Seated* sign.

"I don't know," Dez said carefully. "I think there are some women who've been able to break through that."

Frankie scoffed. "First of all, if you mention Ayn Rand, I swear to God I'm going to kill you in your sleep."

Dez idly wondered if that was a veiled promise to share her bed tonight.

"Two for dinner?" the hostess said. She was skinny, her strawberry blonde hair was big, and she smelled of Aqua Net.

"Dessert," Dez said. The hostess put the dinner menus away and grabbed the smaller dessert menus.

Dez and Frankie, led by the ozone-depleting scent of hairspray, followed the hostess to an empty table and sat.

"You can pick up a Tom Clancy or a Dean Koontz and expect all kinds of stuff," Frankie went on. "But you won't get that with a Nora Roberts or a Ngaio Marsh."

"Toni Morrison?"

Frankie got a thoughtful look on her face. "Honestly, if anyone can break it, she can. But she's got the, uh..."

"Racism thing?" Dez ventured.

"I was going to say something like 'the weight of a wrongful history' behind her. And her books make you uncomfortable because she's talking about something that Stephen King and Tom Clancy can't."

Dez nodded, although she wasn't sure she really agreed.

"My point is," Frankie said, trying to maintain the head of steam she'd built up, "you'd never pick up a Francesca Bethany novel if you've heard it reads like the next blood-soaked Schwarzenegger screenplay."

"I guess a lot of people might not," Dez said. Was that her first name? Francesca?

The waitress came over and introduced herself with a name Dez immediately forgot.

"Just dessert tonight?" she asked.

Dez nodded.

"The cheesecake is our specialty," the waitress said, "But we also have an excellent peach cobbler. Those are the two most popular items on the menu, and I've got to tell you, honestly, they're my favorites."

Dez looked at Frankie. "What do you think, girl? One of each?"

Frankie shrugged. "That's fine."

"Do you like something else better here?"

"No," Frankie replied noncommittally. "The cheesecake's good. It's worth it."

"Okay," Dez said, recognizing that Frankie was playing a game—but she couldn't figure out which one. Nor did she really want to participate. "One of each of those, and a coffee for me, please. Frankie, you want coffee?"

"No, I'll be up all night."

The waitress nodded, gathered their menus, and walked away.

"So," Dez said, "how come you let them get away with that?"

"Get away with what?"

"With, uh, I don't know how to say it. *Forcing your conformity.* Your agent, your readers, anyone. Come on, this is supposed to be the decade of the woman, right? Hillary Clinton campaigning alongside Bill, Oprah making movies, woman CEOs? You're bending to the agent just because you're not a romance writer?"

Frankie sniffed. "Spoken like someone who's never written a book before."

Dez laughed. "Well, girl, you got me there."

"And another thing," Frankie said. "I don't have to be a romance writer to make money."

"But if you're not, you have to be male."

Frankie began to bristle. "Listen, it was *my* decision. I don't have to defend it to you."

Dez gave Frankie a tired smile. "Of *course* not. I'm just saying. That's not giving your public much credit. This is a different world than it was when George Eliot or Jane Austen were writing. It's even a different world than Ayn Rand wrote in."

Frankie closed her eyes and shook her head.

"Oh, Lord, Frankie, don't kill me in my sleep over *that.*"

Frankie still didn't smile, but she sighed and sat back.

The waitress appeared with their desserts and two spoons for each of them. "And your coffee will be right up. They're just brewing a fresh pot."

Frankie looked at the waitress walk away. "Think she'd still serve us if she knew we were two girls out on a date?"

Dez leaned back in the booth. "I guess it depends on how she feels about it. My senior year, a girl wanted to bring another girl to senior prom. She was very vocal. A few of the parents threatened to boycott. But I was amazed—the school let her do it."

"That's not that big of a deal. Schools here have been allowing that for a while."

"Yeah, but this was in Lake Charles, Louisiana. They usually just sweep all that shit under the rug. But I think maybe only four or five parents pulled their kids out of the prom and asked for a refund of their tickets."

"So were you the girl?"

Dez shook her head. "Sometimes I *wish* I'd been that girl. I might not have run away from Lake Charles to California."

"You ran away?"

"Not like a teenaged runaway. I graduated high school and applied to schools on the West Coast. Ran my ass off in track to get a scholarship."

Frankie's eyes went to Dez's body. Dez thought perhaps Frankie would make a comment about Dez having a runner's body, but her outfit didn't reveal anything about her shape or athleticism. Well, her jeans looked good on her, but she was sitting and the table was in the way.

"And you came out here, huh?"

"Yes ma'am," Dez said. "I have an aunt who lives out in Bakersfield. Makes Thanksgiving and Christmas a little easier."

Frankie nodded, but Dez could tell she wasn't paying very close attention. Dez took one of the spoons and started to take a spoonful from the point of the cheesecake.

"Wait!" Frankie said quickly, holding up her hand.

Dez paused, her spoon in mid-air. "What?"

"My mother always used to say that if you ate cheesecake backwards—from the crust to the point— then you can make a wish before you eat the point and it will come true."

Dez smiled. "You don't strike me as the superstitious type."

Frankie smiled back. "I've never had a wish come true yet, but it doesn't mean I don't do it."

"I never heard of that before."

"It's because you've got voodoo in Louisiana. It's probably a totally different set of superstitions."

Dez let her Louisiana drawl come out. "You best be careful, Miss Frankie, you don't want me puttin' no curse on you or nothin'."

Frankie laughed, a full, open-mouthed, hearty laugh, but Dez immediately felt pangs of regret for going into that mode.

She and Rhonda would riff on their backgrounds constantly, putting on their mothers' accents. On weekend nights, if neither one of them had a date—which wasn't often for Rhonda, but was quite often for Dez—they'd grab a case of cheap beer or, God forbid, wine coolers, grab burritos at the local *taquería*, turn on an old cheesy movie, and start to make fun of their families, especially with their accents and their half-English phrases (Rhonda called her mother's odd phrasings *Nicaraglish*), and the passive-aggressive things their mothers would do to try to assure that Dez and Rhonda would end up with good husbands. It was cathartic, and Dez and Rhonda often collapsed in gales of laughter, talking over the television, pleasantly buzzed, maybe even braving the traffic on Stearns and Los Coyotes to walk to In-N-Out for cheeseburgers. And now Dez had pulled back the curtain to a stranger, a white girl at that. And maybe she wasn't even a lesbian.

"I'll be right back," Frankie said, wiping her mouth with the off-white cloth napkin. "Don't eat the point of the cheesecake while I'm gone." She shook her finger at Dez and flitted off.

Dez watched her walk away, toward the restrooms, admiring her figure. When Frankie turned the corner,

Dez leaned forward and took a spoonful of peach cobbler. The peaches weren't fresh, but she wasn't sure what she expected in late January.

Frankie had left her purse on the table. For a fleeting moment, Dez pictured herself rifling through Frankie's purse to find out her real name. Was Bethany really her middle name? Was her last name something long and unpronounceable? Lord knows Dez had enough Californians mispronounce *her* last name. Or was it something pedestrian, like Smith or Jones or Johnson?

She took another bite of cheesecake, eating it backward, like Frankie's mother would have wanted, leaving the point untouched.

She thought back to the last date she had been on, just when the school year started, with a very out lesbian who was loud and proud. Her date went by the name Mettie, although Dez found out that it was really Margaret. Partially shaved head and a man's tee shirt with the sleeves ripped off that said *Stormé*. Like with Frankie, everything out of her mouth was a diatribe. Frankie was all about gender dynamics in literature, and Mettie was all about sexual dynamics in culture and society. And Mettie was *very* sexual, as she let most of the people in the restaurant know. It had been a typical Southern California September, with the Santa Ana winds making Long Beach blazing hot for a week at a time before cooling down to something tolerable for a day or two. It had been one of the hotter days, and Dez had worn a tank top and shorts, and Mettie had been very vocal about liking Dez's runner's body, enough to make Dez uncomfortable.

Mettie had driven Dez home and had been very clear, and quite descriptive, in her goals for the rest of the evening. Dez had politely declined, wondering if Mettie would take no for answer. She wasn't happy about it, but she had left Dez at the door and hadn't called again.

Dez sighed, eating another bite of cheesecake. She had eaten almost half of it, and should probably leave some for Frankie. Although Frankie might so busy 'speechifying' the rest of the night, as Dez's mother would say, that she might not notice that the whole slice of cheesecake was gone. As long as the point was left.

Dez wondered if the evening could be saved. The whole Frank Bethany thing was intriguing. How does someone make the decision to do that? What makes them tick? And Dez knew that her physical attraction to Frankie had a lot to do with her willingness to stick it out until the end of the date. But Dez thought Frankie probably wasn't interested enough to continue. Not unless something changed when Frankie got back from the restroom.

She looked up from her reverie and Frankie appeared, sliding easily back into her chair—and immediately noticed that the cheesecake was half-eaten. "Well, I see *someone* likes the cheesecake," she said, giggling.

"Yeah, the waitress was right. It's really good." Dez thought Frankie's laughter was potentially a good sign.

Frankie stuck her lower lip out in a mock pout. "But that same someone doesn't like the peach cobbler."

"The peaches aren't fresh," Dez said. Frankie was in a good mood compared to when they were walking to the bistro, but it was a little suspicious. Dez looked in Frankie's eyes, and couldn't tell in the low light of the bistro if her eyes were unusually dilated.

"Well, what did you expect? It's January."

Dez nodded. "Sure."

"I see you've been eating the cheesecake backward." She smiled, a little goofily, and took Dez's hand in hers. "Thank you for respecting me and my family." She guffawed, then grabbed her spoon, scooped up the point of the cheesecake, and shoveled it in her mouth.

Dez stared at her.

"Ha, ha," Frankie said with her mouth full.

"I can't believe you just did that," Dez said.

"I know," Frankie said around the bite of cheesecake. "I didn't even make a wish."

4

FRANKIE'S GOOD MOOD DIDN'T DISSIPATE. SHE TALKED about how much she loved *Die Hard*, and how the whole movie was a multilayered critique of Reaganomics. Dez didn't believe it at first, but she explained it so well, so thoroughly, and with such conviction that Dez finally agreed, breaking into a smile.

Dez paid the bill, though as a college student, the idea of taking out a bestselling author was a little annoying. Still, Dez reasoned, she had been the one to ask Frankie out. And it was coffee and dessert, not a full steak and lobster dinner. Although that would have been better than the Whopper Jr. she had called a meal.

The rain had come back when they left the bistro, but it was just drizzling.

"You want to chance it?" Frankie said in Dez's ear. And Dez felt the tingle of attraction with Frankie, the same as she had when Frankie was in the dress with the cherries at the party in Westwood. The anger about the unfairness of the publishing industry seemed miles away. Even Frankie eating the point of the cheesecake seemed spontaneous and edgy, not obnoxious or bitchy. Although Dez wasn't sure how much that opinion was affected by Frankie's tight sweater.

And there was the suspicious, dramatic change before and after Frankie's visit to the bathroom—but Dez decided not to look a gift horse in the mouth.

"Sure, we can chance it," Dez said. "It's not bad. And it's only about a half-mile." Ten minutes, tops, even if they walked slowly.

But when they got a block away from the bistro, the skies completely opened and it started to pour. Frankie squealed, the way she might have if she had been on a date with a boy, and Dez took her hand and they started to run like schoolgirls, splashing through the rain on the sidewalk and soaking their feet in the huge puddle next to the curb as they began to cross Sepulveda.

"I can't believe how much it's raining," Frankie said, delight in her voice.

And Dez would have been upset at the rain if it hadn't been for Frankie's sudden turn in mood and her joy at everything that was happening. This was how she remembered Frankie at the party, not the humorless woman of earlier this evening.

They arrived back at Frankie's apartment, laughing and soaking wet, and still holding hands. Frankie fumbled to get the key out of her purse, finally letting go of

Dez's hand, but just long enough to get the door open. She grabbed Dez's hand again as she crossed the threshold, and closed the door behind her with her foot.

Then pulled Dez close, and kissed her hard on the mouth.

Dez kissed back.

"Do you want to get out of those wet clothes?" Frankie asked, breathlessly, although it was more like a statement. Dez nodded and kissed Frankie's neck. They both dropped their purses on the floor, next to the staircase. Frankie started to unbutton Dez's Oxford shirt.

They stumbled to the bedroom.

———————•◆•———————

They held each other for a few minutes after they were done, and Frankie giggled, holding Dez and squeezing her.

"I liked that a lot," she said.

"That was really nice," Dez agreed, although it hadn't been.

"Can I tell you a secret?" Frankie asked.

Dez knew what was coming. "What?"

"When I said I'd been with a woman before. I haven't. You're my first."

Dez nodded, unsurprised.

"I mean, I've kissed girls before, and I've done some other stuff. But that was the first time I've really, you know, *been* with a woman."

Dez nodded again.

Frankie propped herself up on one elbow. "Oh no. You could tell."

Dez shrugged. "I mean, I guess so. But it's okay."

"Are you sure? You don't hate me for lying to you?"

"There was a first time for me, too, you know. It wasn't that long ago. A few years, I guess, but it's not like I've got decades of experience."

Frankie was silent for a minute.

"Like, I bet the first story you ever wrote wasn't as good as *Exodus Nights*."

Frankie laughed. "No. Of course not."

"But I bet you couldn't have written *Exodus Nights* without writing that first story. Just like you need your first time with a girl."

Frankie nodded and flopped on her back. "True enough."

"What *was* the first thing you ever wrote, Frankie?"

She paused. "The first thing I ever wrote. Like, are we talking about elementary school?"

Dez laughed. "How about the first thing you wrote once you knew you wanted to be a writer?"

Frankie chuckled. "Well, that's easy. It was a short story called *The Harbor*."

"That sounds interesting already," Dez said. "I like harbors. Have you been to the Cabrillo Aquarium near San Pedro Harbor?"

"Ugh, aquariums. They're so dark and creepy."

"No, they're not. I love aquariums."

"Fish prisons, you mean."

Dez cleared her throat. "Anyway, your story. What was it about?"

"It's kind of embarrassing."

"Oh now, it can't be as embarrassing as telling me I'm your first girl," Dez said.

"Okay," Frankie said. "It was about this guy. He was really mysterious, you know?" She shifted in the bed until her head was on Dez's shoulder. "I tried all these tricks that they teach you in high school creative writing classes."

"They offered creative writing at your high school?"

"Yeah. They didn't at yours?"

"Nope." Dez took Frankie's hand and intertwined their fingers. "Y'all are lucky. What was a trick you used?"

Frankie chuckled and cuddled into Dez's shoulder. "He had a nervous tic. He'd snap his fingers whenever he was cold. So I alluded to it three times, just like you're supposed to. And—have you heard of Chekhov's Gun?"

"Chekhov's gun? You'd think they've have told me about it in Criminal Justice by now," Dez joked.

"Oh, it's not a real gun. It's a dramatic principle."

Dez closed her eyes. Frankie, even when she was in a good mood, slipped into condescension easily. Dez supposed it was an innocent enough mistake to make, but it still rubbed her the wrong way.

"If you show a gun in act one, you have to fire it by act three," Frankie continued. "Otherwise, why show it in act one?"

"Gotcha."

"I mean, it was *very* formulaic."

"That can work, though," Dez said.

"I guess." Frankie shifted to get more comfortable. "Anyway, the story starts by following this sexy Parisian woman. What was her name? Elantra? Electra? Something like that. It was very un-French. And this insane East German who was paranoid. I wrote this while the Wall was still up, so it had more international intrigue."

"That's very John Le Carré of you," Dez said drily, hoping that Frankie would notice her reference. She had gone through a Le Carré phase during her freshman year, and had bought a few of his obscure novels, her reward for a successful hunt in used bookstores.

"Hah," Frankie said, without humor. Dez couldn't get a read on how she was supposed to take that. "Anyway, this guy—"

"Wait, the East German?"

"No, the guy with the nervous tic. He's a handsome American."

"Well, *obviously*."

"Right. So he and the sexy French chick meet at this leather bar in Soho."

"A leather bar in Soho?"

Frankie laughed. "I know. Ridiculous."

"Soho in London or New York?"

"Does it matter?"

"New York is less ridiculous."

Frankie laughed again, a full throaty laugh, and kissed Dez on the cheek. Dez tried to turn into it, to kiss her on the lips, but Frankie was quick and it was just a peck. "I did say it was the first thing I ever wrote."

"You also said it was embarrassing."

"And it is, right?"

"Oh, yes, indeed. I feel like I got my money's worth."

"So, yes, it's a leather bar in Soho. And they have a conversation—and it's totally stilted, I had absolutely no idea what I was doing with dialogue back then—about the microfilm for the nuclear weapons."

"Microfilm."

"Oh yes. I was very low tech. No floppy disks for me."

"Go on."

"So she says she wants it, and he says he doesn't have it but he knows where it is, and then they just start kissing, passionately, up against the brick wall, and then go into the back room and just have the raunchiest, nastiest sex I could think of at the time."

Dez laughed. "How raunchy and nasty was it?"

Frankie turned red, all the way to the tips of her ears. "Well, considering I had absolutely no idea what I was doing, and considering how *little* experience I had, it wound up being, uh, how can I say this—unintentionally humorous."

"Sounds painful."

"Not as painful as what the sexy French chick did to him when they got on the bed," Frankie said. "My guy friends at the time all cringed when they came to that part. One of them actually said, 'Do you actually think that's sexy? Because if you do, you need to see a shrink.'"

Dez shook her head and smiled. "This sounds *awesome*. You were into some crazy shit way before *Exodus Nights*, huh?"

Frankie giggled. "Okay, now shh, I'm about to get to the good part."

"We're not at the good part yet?"

"Not even close. So just when they both reach the, uh, pinnacle of their excitement, the door bursts open and the sexy Parisian girlfriend's boyfriend comes in and threatens the nervous tic guy with a knife."

"What kind of knife?"

Frankie rolled her eyes. "Well, I don't know, Dez. A *sharp* knife. Right next to his, you know, private area."

"Please," Dez said, "I know I'm a lesbian, but you can use the real words in front of me. I'm not going to shrivel up and die."

"His *penis*, then, Dez, are you happy?" Frankie untwined her fingers from Dez and poked her playfully in the ribs.

Dez smiled, running her fingers through Frankie's hair. "Yes. I'm happy."

"And then," Frankie said, plowing ahead, "just as he's about to cut off the guy's manhood—"

"Manhood?"

"—the East German paranoid guy comes in with a crossbow and nails the boyfriend right between the shoulder blades."

"With a damn crossbow?"

"Not just a crossbow," Frankie said, making flourishing movements dramatically with her hand. "A *silver-tipped arrow.*"

"Was the boyfriend a vampire?"

"Um," Frankie said pensively, "I don't think so. I don't think I was in my vampire-fetish stage at that point."

"Right."

Dez could feel her left arm start to fall asleep. "So what was the verdict?"

"What do you mean?"

"I mean did it get published?"

Frankie laughed. "Oh, no. Not even close. Some of the rejection letters I got were pretty righteous, though."

"Oh, I'm sorry."

"Do *not* be sorry about the failure of *The Harbor*. It was the tenth rejection letter I got before someone told me that the integration of harbor, in both a literal or metaphorical way, made absolutely no sense in the story."

Dez laughed. "Did you hide the symbolism a little too well?"

Frankie shook her head and her hair moved back and forth on Dez's shoulder, tickling her collarbone. "I got so involved with the plot—making sure the East German's descent into madness made sense, making sure that Electra or whatever her name was had a good sense of empowerment, that maybe I didn't spend as much time explaining the meaning of the harbor. But the symbolism was anything but hidden."

Dez wrapped Frankie's hair around her finger.

"And the harbor was actually this really *powerful* allegory. Well, in my young, naïve mind it was really powerful."

"Allegory, huh?"

"Yeah. I had it all figured out. The water represented Jesus, but the piers were going to represent organized religion."

"And just how did you think you were going to pull that off?"

"Well, obviously I never figured that out. But in the big fight scene—in the outline, it happened on the pier itself—the East German and the handsome American were fighting, and ostensibly it was over the affections of the Parisian woman, who represented the future, but the slats on the wharf broke because the pier couldn't handle the demands of the people it was trying to hold up, and because the logs used in construction were rotted from the inside out."

"That sounds a bit heavy-handed."

Frankie scoffed. "Believe me, I've written the most obvious symbolism and nobody gets it. The only people who get it are reviewers, who think everything is too obvious although it goes right over everybody else's head."

"Really?"

"Really. Like—okay, after her two lovers fall into the water, the Parisian woman drove off the pier into the water, and as she's beginning to drown, her mouth fills not with water, but with red wine, and she thinks about how the promise of the pier had led her to this place, how it had led her to transform herself from a human with hopes and dreams into nothing but a corpse in the bottom of the harbor."

"And that's the Jesus metaphor."

"Well, yeah, the harbor, not the Parisian chick. You know the whole water-into-wine thing."

"Yeah, I heard the story once or twice growing up." Dez hoped the sarcasm was evident in her voice—her mother had dragged her to church every Sunday until Dez left for California. "But it didn't get published?"

Frankie sighed and intertwined her fingers with Dez's again. "No. Not even a bite."

Dez smiled. "It might not have worked in that story, but it's actually not a bad metaphor. Maybe you could use it in your next book."

Frankie went quiet, her mouth forming a thin line.

"You okay?"

"I'm just thinking," Frankie said. Her voice was miles away.

Dez lifted her head just enough to pull the pillow down a little. There was no use denying that Frankie was fascinating, and she was coy and cute and curvy—and maddening.

"Hey, listen, Frankie, I've got class in—" Dez grabbed her watch off the nightstand and looked at it. "Oh jeez, six hours. How is it three in the morning?"

Frankie was shaken out of her stupor. "Wait—you have class?"

"Yeah, at nine."

"Aren't you an art director or something?"

Dez shook her head. "Maybe that was the other hot black girl you had sex with." She laughed, but Frankie still had a serious look on her face.

"Did you tell me you were a student?"

Dez was annoyed; she remembered telling Frankie about her track scholarship at the bistro. But she shrugged and gave Frankie an out. "I don't know. We might have been too busy talking about books."

Frankie sat up, the sheets falling down from her shoulders to around her waist. Dez tried not to stare. "Are you a grad student?"

Dez smirked. "Oh, you're afraid you're robbing the cradle now?"

Frankie looked worried.

"How old did you think I was?"

"I don't know," Frankie said. "You like talking about books. You knew all the words to a bunch of eighties songs. I guess I thought you were twenty-five or twenty-six."

"Twenty-five-year-olds can have class in the morning."

"Are you twenty-five?"

Dez laughed. "Nope. Twenty-one."

"You're only twenty-one?"

"Twenty-two in April."

"What were you doing at that party in Westwood?"

Dez leaned over and grabbed her panties and bra and started putting them on under the covers. "Dancing with you to 'Tainted Love.'"

"Where are you going?"

"Home. To get some sleep."

"No, I mean where are you going to school?"

"Oh. Cal State Long Beach." Dez realized, perhaps too late, that they had spent almost all evening talking about Frankie. Frankie's book, Frankie's story, Frankie's opinions on gender dynamics, Frankie's opinions on authorship, Frankie Frankie Frankie. Perhaps the only thing that Frankie knew about Dez was that she liked cheesecake. Well, and that Dez could do that one thing with her fingers and her tongue at the same time.

"What are you studying?"

Dez looked at Frankie. Her face was open, her eyes wide. Was she making up for lost time on the date, just now realizing that she had monopolized the conversation? Dez got out of bed and realized her annoyance was growing. But she smiled, the widest, most sincere smile she could hope for. "Oh, come on, Frankie, we won't have anything to talk about on our next date." She picked up her jeans, still damp from the rain, and put them on.

That put Frankie off balance and she wasn't sure how to respond. Finally she smiled. "Right. And I have writing to do tomorrow too."

"You okay dating a younger woman?" Dez put her shirt on and began to button it up.

Frankie smiled. "Sure. It just surprised me, is all."

Dez smoothed her shirt down and looked around. "Did I leave my purse downstairs?"

"I don't know," Frankie said. "Let me go pee. I'll see you out."

Dez went downstairs. She put her black Doc Martens on, still wet from the rain, but dry inside. She saw her purse—next to Frankie's on the floor.

She thought briefly for a moment, then opened Frankie's purse and pulled out the wallet. Frankie's wallet was leather-edged but made of canvas, with a floral pattern, blue and lavender and purple. Dez thought of the red cherry dress and how good a dress in the same fifties-pinup cut would look on Frankie with the wallet's floral pattern. She looked at the driver's license.

It was from New Hampshire.

Jennifer Renée Morgenstern.

Dez was stunned and almost dropped the wallet.

She checked again—but the photo next to the name was definitely Frankie's. She wanted to go through every inch of the wallet. She pulled out a MasterCard, also reading *Jennifer R Morgenstern.*

What was going on? Was this a trick? She started to look at other cards in the wallet, but she heard the toilet flush upstairs.

She put everything back in the wallet and put the wallet back in the purse, leaving it right where she'd found it—at least, as close as she could remember. She and Frankie—or whoever she was—were making out when they dropped their purses, so she doubted Frankie would notice if anything were slightly out of place.

Footfalls on the stairs.

Dez blinked hard, trying not to have a shocked look on her face. She was tired—it was a little after three in the morning, after all—and the adrenaline rush from the sex had worn off. She realized she had at least a thirty-minute drive ahead of her, too, and suddenly a wave of exhaustion hit her.

Frankie appeared. She had put on a nightie, a little frilly, a little see-through; something Dez would never have been caught dead in.

"Are you sure you don't want to spend the night?" Frankie said. "My bed is nice and warm. It would be nice to be with someone else on a rainy night like this."

The nightie was meant to keep her there, Dez knew—and if she hadn't opened up the wallet and seen a name that had nothing to do with *Frank Bethany*, she might have stayed. Actually, Dez admitted to herself, she *definitely* would have stayed.

"I don't want to fight traffic from Torrance and run the risk of being late for class," Dez said. "Plus it'll take an hour and a half in the morning. It'll only take thirty minutes now."

"Okay," Frankie said. She stepped closer to Dez, but Dez didn't step closer to her. "Um," she said. "I've never done this with a girl. Do we, like, kiss goodbye?"

Dez leaned over and kissed Frankie on the mouth. Dez started slow but Frankie returned the kiss passionately, moaning a little, in a very sensual way that Dez guessed Frankie's male lovers would find irresistible.

Dez broke the kiss first. "Bye," she said. "I'll call you."

She opened the door. The rain had continued falling heavily, but Dez was glad to get out of the apartment.

She stepped out into the downpour and a sense of calm came over her.

She walked out to the car, getting soaked, feeling Frankie's eyes on her. She turned; Frankie was standing in the doorway in her thin, lacy nightie. Dez lifted her hand to wave goodbye.

Dez got in the car and sat for a few seconds, breathing hard. Warning bells, red flags, bridge out signs—everything was telling her to drive home and never look back.

She could still get four hours of sleep and be in the library for an hour before class tomorrow.

5

Dez found what she was looking for in a 1986 article in *The Dartmouth*. The microfiche made the photograph a series of white blobs on the reader's screen, but there it was: *Prof. Bethany Nominated for PEN Award.*

And even through the white blob, Dez could see that Professor Bethany was a real person, a man with a confident smile and strong jaw, and that he was not a cute curvy white girl.

"You sure can pick 'em, Dez," she mumbled to herself. She rubbed her eyes and started reading the article.

English department professor Frank Bethany has been nominated for the prestigious PEN/Faulkner award for fiction for his debut novel, "Exodus Nights," published in June 1985. His second novel, "Friendly Fire," has a release date of early 1987.

"Exodus Nights" is the first debut novel to be nominated in the five-year history of the award. Bethany will compete with Tobias Wolff, Harriet Doerr, and other authors. The award will be presented in April at the Folger Shakespeare Library in Washington, D.C.

She had expected the article to be longer, perhaps continued on another page, but that was it. She scanned through the rest of that week's edition: an article on a professor's sponsored trip to West Berlin, the opening of a new dormitory planned for the fall quarter, and the injury of the star lacrosse forward. Dez had spun the wheel back to the beginning when she saw it.

On the masthead, in the list of staff writers, *Jen Morgenstern*. Dez narrowed her eyes and thought for a bit, then realized she was going to be late for class if she didn't get going.

That evening, Dez walked home through the rain with her hood pulled over her head. She hadn't been able to pay attention in class, the lecture on interviewing witnesses just an audial jumble in her mind. She wondered what else Frankie had done to perpetuate the ruse. Was she pretending to be the famous author just in front of Dez, or was this the persona she presented to the world?

The telltale mud tracks, still wet in front of the door, suggested that Rhonda was home. Rhonda had, unsurprisingly, been asleep when Dez finally got home at 3:45 that morning, and had left for her morning class before Dez woke up. Dez stifled a yawn—after only four hours of sleep, she was exhausted, and walked upstairs, stopping in front of Rhonda's open door. Rhonda was on her computer playing Minesweeper.

"Hey, girl," Rhonda said, not taking her eyes off the screen.

"Hey, Rhonda."

"You got in late."

"Sorry. Didn't mean to wake you."

"How was your date with the *chela*?"

Dez hesitated.

"Oh, come on, Dez. You were out too damn late to *not* have a good time." She clicked and a bomb appeared. "Dammit."

"Well," Dez said. "She had, uh, she was..."

"She was what? Unshowered?" Rhonda started a new game.

"Inexperienced with girls."

Rhonda shook her head. "Oh, *no*. What was she doing at that party in Westwood?"

"I'm not sure. I guess she's looking for a change."

"You cut your hair different if you want a *change*. You don't start having sex with girls."

"Oh, come on now, Rhonda. Be a little nice. Remember *your* first time with a girl."

Rhonda pressed her lips together and didn't say anything.

"Yeah," Dez continued, "you remember how awkward and weird it was, don't you?"

"Fine," Rhonda said, "you made your point. But you're avoiding the question."

Dez crossed her arms and tapped her foot, debating what to say. "You ever been with someone who didn't tell you their real name?"

Rhonda stopped playing and looked at Dez. "What do you mean, didn't tell you their real name? *Frankie* isn't her real name?"

Dez shook her head. "No. It's *Jennifer Morgenstern.*"

"She tell you that?"

Dez looked at the floor and pursed her lips.

"Oh my God, you naughty ho. You went through her purse. You went through her purse!"

"Well, I did—"

"Before or after you had sex with her?"

Dez put a hand over her face.

"After?" Rhonda sputtered. "You have sex with her and you didn't even know her real name?"

"Well, I do now," Dez offered lamely.

Rhonda stopped. "So does she have a reason for calling herself Frankie? Is there, I don't know, some favorite uncle, or a childhood nickname or something?"

"I dunno."

"Well, I'm just saying, it might not be as, uh, *evil* as you think it is."

"Now, hold on, I don't think it's *evil.*"

"Yes you do," Rhonda said. "I can see it all over your face. You think she's pulling one over on you. You think she's a drug dealer or something. That she's putting cocaine into a blister on the bottom of a boat and that you're going to have to go all Sonny Crockett on her ass."

"No, girl, that's crazy."

"Okay, fine, whatever," Rhonda said, holding her hands out in front of her. "You can lie to yourself. *I* know you think that something's going on."

Dez was quiet for a moment. "Fine," she said slowly and carefully, "tell me how it's *not* a bad thing."

"Okay," Rhonda said. "Let me tell you a story. I had this friend in elementary school. Knew her since kindergarten. And she totally loved Kermit the Frog."

"Sure." Dez cracked her knuckles. "Lots of kids love Kermit."

"Yeah," Rhonda said, "but she took it pretty far. She made a necklace out of green felt triangles, just like Kermit has, and she wore it every day. And one day, I think it was in second grade, this new kid just started calling her 'Kermit,' thinking he was making fun of her. I was right next to her at the time, eating my lunch, and her eyes got super-big and just lit up. I asked her what she was thinking, and she just had this faraway look in her eyes. I said her name." She paused. "Damn, I can't even think what her real name is now. Maybe it was *Amy*. And she said, 'I'm not Amy, I'm *Kermit*.'" And she wouldn't let anyone call her Amy after that. She just refused to answer. The teacher wigged out for a little while, but then she just went with it too."

"So what cartoon character is named Frankie?"

"Well, shit, I don't know, Dez. Maybe she likes Frankie Avalon or Frankie Goes to Hollywood or Frank N. Furter from *Rocky Horror*."

Dez shifted her weight. "Yeah, I actually wouldn't be surprised if she liked *Rocky Horror*." She tapped her chin. "Though she's way more of a Janet."

"What did she say about her name?"

Dez was quiet again.

"Of course you didn't ask her about it," Rhonda said. "You'd rather think the worst about someone then give them a chance to explain."

Dez started to object.

"Sorry, sorry, sorry," Rhonda said. "That came out wrong. I just meant that, well, you're not the most, uh, *trusting* person in the world. You're kind of, I don't know, a pessimist."

Dez smiled. "Well, sure, I'm a pessimist. But her name's got nothing to do with Frankie Goes to Hollywood or *Rocky Horror*."

Rhonda shrugged. "What, then?"

"She said she wrote novels under a pen name. Frank Bethany."

Rhonda's mouth was agape. "Frank Bethany?"

"You know him?"

"Ugh. My brother will *not* shut up about him. He was bugging me to read that one. You know, the famous one. *Genesis* something."

"*Exodus Nights*."

Rhonda snapped her fingers. "Right. So you *do* know who that is."

"Well, not really. I just picked up *Exodus Nights* last night before our date. I hadn't heard of him before."

Rhonda stood up. "Do you think it's true? Do you think this Jennifer chick actually wrote *Exodus Nights*? Do you think you could get a book signed? My brother would totally lose his mind."

Dez shook her head. "I think it's a lie. I, uh, I did a little research this morning."

"When did you have time to do research?"

Dez shifted her weight uncomfortably. "I went to the library before class. Frank Bethany is actually an English professor at Dartmouth."

"You are *such* a stalker! I can't believe it. Dartmouth? Like, the Ivy League school?"

"Yeah," Dez said. "And Jennifer Morgenstern was on the newspaper staff there."

"Well," Rhonda said. "That's weird."

Dez nodded. "Yes, it's weird. That's exactly what I was thinking. I think something happened at Dartmouth."

"What's she doing in L.A. if she went to Dartmouth?"

"I don't know. That was six years ago."

"Oh," Rhonda winked. "An *older* woman."

"She's not that much older."

"Six years? That's what? Twenty-eight?"

"Maybe. She might have been a freshman six years ago."

"Or maybe she was a grad student. Who held the walker while you were doing it?"

"Shut up, Rhonda. *You* saw the way she looked in that red-and-white cherry dress."

Rhonda nodded. "I sure did. You're lucky she was so into you. I kinda wanted her to myself."

Dez sighed. "Lucky? Rhonda, she's lying about who she is. I'd've been lucky if *you* had gone out with her instead of me. You probably would have called her on her Frank Bethany bullshit."

"Maybe she's playing with you. Maybe she's trying to see how well-read you are."

"Yeah, well, maybe she's a psychopath."

Rhonda paused. "Hah. Maybe she's a psychopath." She sat back down and clicked. It was a bomb. "Dammit." She started the game over. "You gonna see her again?"

"I don't know. It wasn't great. She talked about herself a lot. A whole lot. And the sex was kind of mediocre."

"Think she can improve?"

"Maybe. Since it was only her first time with a girl."

"She a good kisser?"

Dez thought about it. "Yes."

"Well, then, there's probably hope for her." Rhonda looked toward Dez again. "She been with a man, or is she a total virgin?" Then she stopped herself. "Never mind. There's no way she can look like *that* in that cherry dress and be a virgin. She just needs a good teacher."

"I think she needs more than that. I think she needs lithium."

Rhonda chortled.

"I'm actually going to the bookstore to do some, uh, reconnaissance work. You want to come?"

"I don't know," Rhonda said. "I've got an essay I should probably start."

"When's it due?"

"Next week."

Dez smiled. "That's all kinds of time, Rhonda. Come on. It'll be fun."

"I don't know," Rhonda said again.

"You know you're just going to sit here and play Minesweeper all night if you don't."

"It's raining."

"It'll be an adventure."

Rhonda thought for a minute. "Burritos?"

"Fine," Dez said. "Burritos. Bookstore first, though."

6

DEZ AND RHONDA GOT TO BOOKEARTH FORTY-FIVE
minutes later. The traffic had been bad; there were two
separate accidents on the freeway, both of which looked
like issues from the rain. They walked in; Dez noticed
the same stunning Asian woman—Audrey, *that* was her
name—behind the information desk as the night before.

"I can't believe you convinced me to go out in the rain
when I was safe and dry at home, and spend an hour on
the freeway just to come to a stupid *bookstore*," Rhonda
said, a little too loud. From behind the information desk,
Audrey looked up and gave Rhonda a nasty look.

"This store has the biggest selection in L.A.," Dez
said. "And it's a better use of your time than sitting on
your ass playing computer games. Now shut up and
come help me find it."

"Find what?"

"Anything by Jennifer Morgenstern."

"Did she write under her real name?"

"I don't know, Rhonda. That's what I came here to find out."

They went to the fiction section. The same books by Frank Bethany were on the shelf in the B's—nothing new had come in. They walked to the other side of the row to the M's.

"I don't see anything by Morgenstern," said Rhonda.

"Me neither," Dez said. "Maybe it's in non-fiction. Memoir or something. Or in one of the genre sections— western or horror or something like that."

"Want to split up?" suggested Rhonda. "Why don't you take history and self-help? I'll take western and horror."

"Maybe the bargain fiction," Dez mused, walking back through the shelves to the front of the store.

"Oh, you're okay dragging me all the way out here on a Thursday night, but you're afraid of digging through the history section of the bookstore?"

"Too many white people in the history section," said Dez. "They look at me with either hate or pity."

"Well, *I'm* not going over there," Rhonda said.

"I've got a better idea," said Dez, starting to walk toward the cute girl at the information desk. Rhonda started to follow. "No, no," Dez said, "I'm going to be needing her help. She already doesn't like you because of that bookstore crack you made."

"*Everybody* likes me," Rhonda said with a smirk.

"Just go browse the westerns or horror."

Rhonda walked off toward the horror section mumbling to herself about getting an idea from Dean Koontz about killing Dez as painfully as possible.

Dez walked up to the information desk. Audrey, behind it, cute as she was, was looking warily at her. Dez double-checked her nametag just to make sure this wasn't Audrey's grumpy evil twin.

"Hi," Dez said. "I was in here yesterday, buying Exodus Nights."

"Oh, that's right," Audrey said, brightening. "I remember you. I suppose I didn't recognize you with your, um, friend."

"Yes," Dez said, "I can dress her up, but I can't take her out."

The woman looked at Rhonda, walking from the memoir section to the horror shelves, in her shiny blue Adidas sweatpants and a white muscle shirt, the tattoo of Marilyn Monroe's face clearly visible on her left bicep. The woman smirked. "Doesn't look like you can dress her up, either."

"Hey, come on," Dez said, "that's not nice."

The woman smiled and looked in Dez's eyes. Dez smiled back.

"I'm Audrey," the woman said.

"Hi, Audrey; I'm Desirée." Dez had a moment of shock at the words that just came out of her mouth: she hadn't introduced herself as *Desirée* since junior high.

"That's a pretty name."

"Thanks." Dez could feel the color rise to her cheeks. "Hey, I'm hoping you can help me. There's an author I'm looking for. Can you search the computer for me?"

"Sure," Audrey said, nodding. "Just need the author or title."

"It's Jennifer Morgenstern."

"Morgenstern. M-O-R-G-A-N—"

"I'm pretty sure it's E-N," Dez said, closing her eyes and picturing the New Hampshire driver's license in her head.

"And then S-T-E-R-N?"

"That's what I think," Dez said. "First name Jennifer. Or maybe Jen."

She fell silent as Audrey typed on the keyboard and looked at the small monochrome monitor in front of her.

Dez leaned over a little bit, not so much as to be obnoxious—at least she hoped it wasn't too obnoxious—and looked at Audrey's hands while she typed. Her hands had long, delicate fingers that flew on the keys, the speed almost superhuman. Her fingernails were short and immaculately clean.

Audrey screwed up her mouth on one side. "I only see one title," she said. "It's called *Murder on a Lifeboat*, and it came out about eight years ago." A light bulb went off in Audrey's head. "Hey, you bought *Exodus Nights* yesterday?"

"Yes, I sure did."

"Have you started it yet? Because that starts with a murder on a lifeboat."

"Yeah, I know. I started reading it last night."

"Did it make you think of this book?"

"Sort of," Dez said. "I didn't get it at the time, but I kind of had a brainstorm."

"Well," Audrey said, "it wouldn't have been trying to rip off *Exodus Nights*. It was published before the Bethany book."

"Oh, before?" Dez was interested now. "How much longer before?"

"Well," Audrey started, and then fell silent, squinting at the screen. "It looks like it was about six months. But it was a small press, and it looks like it was a short run. Just a couple of thousand copies."

"You got any copies here?"

Audrey shook her head. "I'm not even sure I could special order it. I could call the publisher, but they're in Boston, and it's well after five o'clock there."

Dez stood back, wondering what she was going to do. "Think I could ask you to call them tomorrow?"

"Of course," Audrey said. "Now, I must warn you, even if they do have a copy or two in their warehouse, you'll probably have to pay full price for the book, plus shipping, and it won't get here for a week or two."

"That's all right."

"I'll need your phone number, Desirée."

"Sure," Dez said.

Audrey opened her desk drawer and got a thick paper bookmark with a large green BookEarth logo on it. "Write it there," she said, and put a pen in front of Dez and held the bookmark down with two hands, her long, delicate, immaculate fingers pinning the edges to the solid surface. Dez would have to put a hand on top of one of Audrey's. *Pretty bold move*, Dez thought. She looked up at Audrey and Audrey was smiling back at her.

Dez put her left hand on top of Audrey's fingers and felt a spark. She looked up in Audrey's eyes, wide open, creased at the corners in a smile. She wrote her name—*Desirée*—between Audrey's hands on the bookmark. And then wrote her phone number.

"I'll call you as soon as I have something on the Jennifer Morgenstern book," Audrey said. Dez took her hands away.

"Thanks," Dez said. "I appreciate it." She took a couple steps back, smiled, and turned to go find Rhonda.

She didn't have very far to go. Rhonda was right behind the first bookshelf.

"Well, look at you, Casanova," Rhonda said in a low whisper. "The ink has barely dried on Frankie and you're putting the moves on the hot Asian chick at the bookstore."

"I was just getting information on an author," Dez said.

"Oh, please," Rhonda said. "You were getting a lot more than that."

They turned and started to walk out of the store.

"Maybe I'm going to have to start hanging out with literary types," Rhonda said. "I never get to meet any hot girls."

"What are you talking about?" Dez said. "You've had a parade of girls leaving your bed every weekend since freshman year. You're as bad as a lot of the guys I know. Worse, even."

"Not every weekend, and it's not a *parade*," Rhonda said. "And a lot of them are like Frankie. They don't know what they want. I think half of them sleep with me because I'm more manly than their last boyfriend was."

Dez cackled.

"All right, are we done with all the book bullshit?" Rhonda said. "I'm dying for a burrito supreme.

7

THE DRIVE HOME FROM THE *TAQUERÍA* WAS EXCRUCIAT-
ing for Dez. She didn't know what to do about Frankie.
Part of her thought Frankie was crazy, the cherries on her
dress turning into red flags. But part of her thought that
Frankie was one of the sanest people she had ever met,
turning the tables on her plagiarist and subsuming his
identity, even if no one would know except her date.

Of course, if Frankie could lie about her name and
her occupation and her writing, she could lie about a
lot more than that. Maybe she was lying about never
being with a woman before. Maybe she'd lie about a lot
of things if Dez started a relationship with her. Maybe
she'd get angry and confrontational if Dez so much as
called her *Jennifer* to her face.

The windshield wipers clicked back and forth. Dez
could hear the quiet but high-pitched clicking even

over the drone of Rhonda's voice. Rhonda was chatty tonight after their burritos, talking about a girl in her women's studies class who was earnest and passionate and curious, who, Rhonda said, looked fantastic in a pair of tight white cutoffs and a plaid flannel shirt.

"I never know anymore," Rhonda complained. "It used to be, you saw a girl in a lumberjack shirt, you could be pretty sure you could ask her out and she'd be open for it. Now, you don't know. She could be gay, sure, or she could just be into Pearl Jam."

"The world is changing all around us," Dez said in half-agreement.

Rhonda continued to talk about the girl in the lumberjack shirt and the mixed signals she was getting all night during their date, but Dez's attention started to wane. She wondered if she should continue reading *Exodus Nights*. She thought it was certainly good enough to keep going with it, although she had to be honest with herself in that she was much more interested in it when she thought Frankie, and not a middle-aged white man, wrote it. Of course, she'd have to see if there was any resemblance between *Exodus Nights* and *Murder on a Lifeboat*. And Dez wasn't sure how much resemblance there had to be. She was reasonably sure Frank Bethany wouldn't execute a word-for-word theft and publish it under his own name. She thought instead there was likely to be thematic similarities, maybe even characters who sounded alike. At the very worst, Dez assumed, there would be a few whole paragraphs or characters or plot lines lifted nearly verbatim, possibly with only a few cosmetic changes—a name, identifying marks, locations, that kind of thing. She shook her head. They hadn't gone through plagiarism or intellectual property theft in any of her classes yet. Dez wasn't even wholly sure it would merit its own set of offenses, much less its own class in her program.

Dez got off the freeway and turned off the frontage road onto Palo Verde. They were less than five minutes from their apartment now. The rain, a constant pounding on the roof of the car throughout the drive, started coming down harder. This was going to be a bad season for mudslides, thought Dez, and she sighed.

"Okay," Rhonda said. "I know you haven't been paying attention to anything I've said for the last ten minutes. Are you seriously that hung up on this girl?"

"I don't know," said Dez.

"Well, stop it," said Rhonda. "I will admit she's hot as hell, but something's going on with her. You don't lie like that—not even her real name, for God's sake—without something being serial-killer level wrong with you."

Dez laughed. "She's not a serial killer."

"You don't know that," Rhonda pointed out. "Lots of serial killers look like normal people."

"I don't think any serial killer has looked like Frankie."

"She is absolutely not worth it," Rhonda said. "You said yourself you were disappointed in the sex.

She might be hot, but it's not worth it if the sex isn't good. It's not even worth it if she's totally *sane* if the sex isn't good."

"I thought you said all she needed was a good teacher."

"Now don't you go changing the subject," Rhonda said. "I know that look. You think you can change her. You think that she's going to get better in the sack once she has a little more Dez under her belt."

Dez tapped her fingers on the steering wheel and didn't say anything.

"You're just as bad as Gabby."

"I am not," Dez said sharply. "Frankie's not abusive."

"You've been on one date," Rhonda said. "But Gabby ignored all the red flags with Dominic, just like you're doing with Frankie. I hate it enough that I have a complete prick for a brother-in-law. I'm not going to see my best friend do the same thing."

"I'm fine," Dez insisted.

"That's what Gabby said too, right when I saw the bruises on her arm."

"There are no bruises on my arm, Rhonda. Back off."

Rhonda held her hands out in front of her. "Sorry, Dez. I call 'em like I see 'em."

"You can stop calling this one."

Rhonda put her hands down as they rolled to a stop at the red light just in front of their apartment complex. "Maybe it's this rain. I'm not used to it. Maybe it's making me cranky."

Dez took her jacket off when she went upstairs and couldn't get the musty, damp smell out of the room. Her jacket wouldn't be able to dry out completely tonight, she knew. Southern California wasn't built for this kind of rain.

She saw *Exodus Nights* on her nightstand.

Dez sighed. She wasn't sure what Frankie or Jennifer was or wasn't, or who she was, or what she did, but it was clear that she was very passionate about the writing of Frank Bethany—whoever *he* was and whatever *he* did. She picked up the book and turned it over, looking for clues. She thumbed through the end pages until she found the acknowledgments, but there was no Jennifer mentioned in the long list of thank yous. Just for good measure, Dez checked for the name Frankie too—no luck.

The call of the book was still strong, however, and she decided to read some more of it before she went to bed. She looked at the clock; it wasn't even nine. She thought about her Friday; she only had one class, and that was at nine o'clock, and there wasn't anything due. She should probably get started on the term paper—it was a class called *Legal Analysis of Police Actions*, which had sounded yawn-inducing, but had become one of the most interesting classes she had taken during her four years at Long Beach. It was a good thing, too; not only did she need it to graduate, but as her only Friday class, it might have been very easy to skip if it weren't so interesting.

She took off her clothes and put on a pair of soft flannel pajamas. They had been in a care package from her mother. She had invited her mother out to visit, hoping to convince her to eventually move, as there was, Dez thought, no future for her in Lake Charles, but a fear of the unknown and an aversion to flying had kept her mother at home.

Once she had her pajamas on, she considered a moment: television—she had missed *The Cosby Show*, but had over an hour before *L.A. Law* came on—but thought that *Exodus Nights* had probably exerted its pull over her enough to win over television this evening.

She called down to Rhonda, who was watching the final scenes of *Martin*, that she was heading to bed. Rhonda shouted something back, but not loud enough for Dez to hear. She assumed it was caustic or sexual in nature. Perhaps it was both; Rhonda was getting skilled at that.

She went into the bathroom, removed her glasses, and took off her makeup. Her face was very close to the mirror, and with her flat nose, wide-set eyes, and dark, short, tightly-curled hair, she wondered what Frankie saw in her. She had purposely made herself less feminine since leaving for college; once she realized that she wasn't the only lesbian on the floor of her dorm, never mind the university—the school actually had a group that met twice a month—she started dressing in jeans and tailored pants, in long-sleeve, button-down Oxford shirts, instead of the dresses, skirts, and blouses her mother had insisted on. She cut her hair close to her head at the beginning of sophomore year; when her mother saw a picture, she almost had a fit, and Dez wasn't sure that the talk about getting closer to her African heritage assuaged her or simply made it worse. But that was when she figured out that her mother suspected.

Dez had once asked Rhonda what had happened when she came out to her parents at the end of her junior year. It had been painful for Rhonda to talk about, and she hadn't said anything the first couple of times. It took a couple of shots of Goldschläger for Rhonda to start talking.

Her father had cut her off with barely a word. Her mother sneaked care packages to her every now and then, and spoke about it being a phase that she'd grow out of. Rhonda had had to apply for financial aid for her tuition and room and board, and working thirty hours a week and going full-time during the summers helped pay for her half of the apartment.

In fact, a lot of the people in the Lambda Support Network group had similar experiences. Many parents had either turned their backs on their children completely or pretended that it wasn't real. Many of the students still hadn't come out to their parents. Some of the ones who did disappeared from school soon after—shipping back home, often to the Central Valley or Imperial Valley, where they would likely move back in with their parents to get "straightened out."

Dez didn't want that life for herself; she didn't want to tell her mother until she had a job and wasn't under her thumb. She really wasn't under her mother's thumb now—her track scholarship was for a full ride, including room and board, which covered the university-owned off-campus apartment she and Rhonda shared. And track didn't start until the spring, although with the wet weather she knew she'd be in trouble if she didn't figure out a way to get going on her sprints soon.

She supposed there wouldn't have been any reason *not* to tell her mom. Except she didn't want to face that. She didn't want to hear the disappointment in her voice, like Rhonda had heard, or the abject denial of what she was, the idea that it was just a phase or something she chose. She remembered in high school, when she stayed home from the prom, how she would have given anything to be attracted to one of the boys on the basketball team or the baseball team or even the chess club. She envied the girl who pushed to take another girl as her date. The thought of herself doing that was frightening—she couldn't even fathom it. And she heard the talk from the school administrators and the parents and the other students, either tut-tutting it, expressing their vocal support—or, like the boys in her English class, graphically expressing their desire to see the two girls go at it.

Dez snapped back to the present. She had been staring into her own eyes in the mirror for far too long.

She shook her head, wiped the excess moisturizer off her hand, and brushed her teeth. She walked back into her room and got an extra pillow from her closet, arranging it on the bed perpendicular to the other pillows, a decent back rest for her to get into a good position to continue reading.

She got into bed, and pulled the covers up, which she rarely had an opportunity to do; it was almost never cold enough. The pounding rain had a dreamy, hypnotic quality to it, and it had been going on so long that it had dipped down into the high forties, almost a record low in Long Beach. She shivered. Southern California had made her soft.

She opened *Exodus Nights* to where she had left off. But it was an almost surreal experience—now reading it with the knowledge that the man in the photograph actually was real, was in fact not a figment of Frankie's imagination, or her uncle. She found the truth far less comforting than the fiction Frankie had made up—and that Dez had, she grudgingly admitted to herself, believed.

Because the thing was, it was a very believable fiction. Dez thought she could discern the female voice in the prose; the lilting rhythms of some of the scenes, as gruesome and as hard to read as they often were.

The chapter ended, and the new chapter started out with criminals who were talking about the bar they were going to rob. When they walked into the bar, Dez pictured the leather bar in Soho from Frankie's first story. She could feel it with all of her senses—she could smell the sweat on the patrons intermingling with the leather, could see the wafting tobacco and marijuana smoke, could hear the loud, high-pitched clacking of the pool balls being struck on the break.

The mirror behind the two robbers shattered, and soon they were racing through the streets on foot with the bouncer chasing them with a shotgun.

And then, as the two men were escaping, they began to have a philosophical conversation. It was about life, it was about their childhoods, it was about their attitudes toward death and sex and food. The first man said they would get away because the bouncer had broken a mirror, and that was seven years of bad luck. The second man began to talk about his childhood in Colombia, and all of the superstitions his *abuelita* followed. Eating twelve grapes at midnight of the new year. Wearing yellow underwear to attract fortune and wealth. Never putting her handbag on the floor.

The first man talked about his aunt, who had always demanded that they eat their pieces of pie backward and save the points for a wish. And then a black butterfly descended down from the sky and flew with them as the two men ran together. The second man turned and ran screaming away from the black butterfly—and was struck by the blast of the shotgun.

Dez set the book down. The story about eating the pie backward wasn't a common practice—or at least, she had never heard of it before. And to hear it coming out of Frankie's mouth and to read it in a Frank Bethany novel within twenty-four hours of each other was too coincidental to be—well, a coincidence.

Had Frankie deliberately told Dez that story, just to see how far she might have been in the novel? There was no way, Dez thought, that Frankie hadn't been aware of the pie story in *Exodus Nights*—and she definitely knew that Dez had started reading it. Was Frankie playing games? Was she just trying to get Dez on her side?

Instead of putting her to sleep, reading *Exodus Nights* had agitated Dez. She swung her legs out of bed and stood up. She paced around the room for a minute, and then went downstairs. Rhonda was still watching television.

"Hey, Dez," Rhonda said, muting the television. "Need me to turn this down?"

"No, it's not that," Dez said. "I just had a real interesting connection between something Frankie said that was supposedly from her childhood, and something I just read in that Frank Bethany book."

"The one that Frankie says she wrote."

"I'm starting to think that maybe the real Frank Bethany plagiarized it from Frankie," Dez said.

Rhonda shook her head. "Listen, Dez, I don't know what's going on with Frankie or Jennifer or whoever she is, but you've gotta see that getting involved in this isn't a good idea, right?"

Dez was quiet.

"This isn't just one or two things that are warning signs, either," Rhonda continued. "This is a guy on the airport runway with those light-up orange flares, crossing them in an X to try to stop you from landing your plane on Frankie's runway."

Dez scoffed. "Well, that's poetic."

"I can fuckin' be Shakespeare when I wanna be," said Rhonda. "My advice is to stay away from Frankie. There's stuff here that will get you in trouble."

Dez looked at the ceiling.

"What is it with you and her, anyway?"

"I don't know," Dez mumbled. "I guess I just find it really interesting. She says a lot of fascinating stuff. She makes me think."

"She introduces you to new authors," Rhonda said sarcastically.

"Girl, shut the hell up," Dez said, but a smile played at the corners of her mouth.

"Seriously," Rhonda said, "you've got enough drama in your life. You don't need to keep pursuing this girl."

"Especially with my super-dramatic roommate."

"I know. So much drama with me bringing home a gorgeous girl every weekend."

"Whatever, Rhonda."

"You know you're just jealous of my game."

Dez smiled and turned to go upstairs. Rhonda looked at the television and unmuted it. The show was back on.

Dez went into her room and climbed into bed, then turned off her reading light. She wanted to think about

Frankie and that cherry dress and her eyes and her lips and the feel of her fingers, but she pushed it out of her mind and turned the pillows around to a more comfortable sleeping position. She sighed. She thought she'd have a lot of trouble falling asleep, especially as she heard the faint sounds of the television from downstairs. But she was asleep within the minute, dreaming of lifeboats, animal transformations, and black butterflies.

8

THE APTLY NAMED DR. ROBERT GALLOWS NEVER FAILED
to remind his students of his previous success as a pros-
ecutor in Los Angeles county. But even his high conviction rate, his many press interviews, and his guest
appearance on a popular cop show failed to fill his
Friday morning class. *Legal Analysis of Police Actions*
needed a better title and time slot. Those students who
signed up for his classes were treated to fascinating if
long-winded stories week in and week out. Dez appre-
ciated the fervor with which Dr. Gallows gave many
of his lectures. The details of many of the cases were
dry, but he injected color and dark humor—"Gallows
humor," as he said with a twinkle in his eye—in the
blandest of cases to make them sing.

Not only that, Dr. Gallows was one of the best legal
minds that Dez had met—although she hadn't met that

many great legal minds. So she decided to stay behind to talk to the professor after class. He preferred the informality of the post-class question-and-answer period to regular office hours, especially on Fridays, when the lecture hall wasn't being used in the ten o'clock hour. Dez preferred it too; some of the professors were downright creepy, especially with the female students, and the open forum was much better—and, Dez thought, safer—than a cramped office where the door could be locked.

There were a couple of students in front of her, and Dez took the time to try to figure out how she was going to frame the question. She stopped and started through a couple of different scenarios, and finally, as the last student in front of her was wrapping up, decided on the direct approach.

"Ah," Dr. Gallows said, "Miss Roubideaux." He pronounced it properly, the French way, with the silent X. Dez was fairly impressed that in a lecture class of a hundred and ten students, he was able to recognize her by sight. Dr. Gallows wasn't very tall—about five foot four, and Dez had about two inches on him—but he was impeccably put together, even on a Friday: a navy Brooks Brothers suit, recently-buffed brown wingtips, a starched white shirt, and, in the only tip-of-the-hat to informality, a J. Garcia tie in an expressionistic crimson and royal blue pattern. It didn't exactly match the suit, but, Dez thought, it was close enough for a Friday college lecture. His hair and full beard were neatly trimmed; the beard, Dez could see up close, hid a weak chin. She found herself wondering if he would even approve of facial hair had he not felt the need to cover up a weakness in his face.

"Hi, Dr. Gallows. I've got a question for you—kind of a practical application question."

"Oh, good, not on the material." Dr. Gallows' eyes lit up. "It's always nice to mix things up a bit. What do you have for me, my dear?"

Dez chose her words carefully. "I've come across a pretty famous novel that I think might have been plagiarized," she said. "And I wonder what, uh, what can be done about it. What might happen to the guy who says he wrote it, and the woman who actually *did* write it."

"Hmm." Dr. Gallows stroked his beard and seemed lost in thought. "Well, Miss Roubideaux, are you asking about criminal charges?"

Dez hesitated.

"Because, as it pertains to this class, I'm not sure there's a lot of relevance to the course material."

"Of course," Dez said quickly. "I mean, I didn't think that there was anything we'd cover in class about this. I just thought—you know, with your background and all..."

"Yes, yes," Dr. Gallows said, absentmindedly. "It's just that I have much more experience with criminal cases than with civil. And, should the author who feels wronged decide to pursue this, it's much more likely that she'll get satisfaction from a civil trial than a criminal one."

"Of course," Dez said again.

"The burden of proof would be on her—your friend," he said.

Dez almost interrupted to say that the author wasn't her friend, but thought better of it.

"And not only would she have to prove that the novel in question was stolen," Gallows continued, "but she'd have to prove that she actually suffered damages—usually financial." He cleared his throat. "It's not enough, either, to determine that the *idea* for a book was taken. It has to be demonstrably proven that it was an idea that was close enough to the final product to be actionable."

"You're saying it's kind of a high bar," Dez said.

Dr. Gallows nodded. "It's meant to be a high bar," he mused. "The United States places a high value on innovation and iteration, and while we have a strong notion of ownership in this country, it must be balanced with the idea that the world is a better place when people build on each other. It isn't the friendliest country in the world to defend intellectual property, though it is better than many. But iterating on good ideas—whether it's the telegraph, the personal computer, or, in this case, perhaps, a novel—is highly valued by the American legal system. So I'd say your friend has a tough row to hoe."

Dez nodded. "Is there a book or something you can recommend? You know, so I can figure out, uh, what to tell my friend?"

Gallows smiled. "The law library has a couple of books on just this sort of thing," he said. "If you can wait until Monday, I can gather a couple of recommendations for you."

"Okay," Dez said, unsure. She was impatient, although she wasn't quite sure why.

"Well," Dr. Gallows said, reading her as easily as he must have been able to read juries in his heyday, "if you can't wait until Monday, the law library is open all weekend. In fact, it might be good for you to do your own research on this. It will teach you to think like a lawyer, and not just rely on the perspective you'll have as a peace officer." Dr. Gallows paused. "You know, as a criminal justice major, you're one of the few students who aren't in the law school or pre-law programs who can even access the law library. You might want to take advantage of it. It will likely give you a leg up when you're applying for law enforcement positions after graduation."

Dez smiled, thanked him, and walked up the steps from the lectern to the exits.

Her head swam as she started to walk back to her apartment. The sky was still gray and foreboding, but the rain had tapered off overnight, and Dez was glad to have the respite. She thought about what she might find in the law library—and then wondered if there had been a case already decided on this topic. Perhaps Jennifer Morgenstern had already brought up a civil case against Frank Bethany. And perhaps if she knew where to look, she could figure it out.

She had been waiting at the light to cross Bellflower Boulevard, but Dez turned right and headed to the law library instead.

"So you've never used LexisNexis before?" the girl behind the law library counter said. She was one of the whitest girls Dez had ever seen, pale skin the color of a new tee shirt, her blonde hair the color of baby powder, with just the subtlest of goldenrod streaks. The girl didn't have a freckle, mark, or blemish anywhere on her face, which made Dez hate her a little bit. She had small features: beady, keen green eyes that kept darting around the room, and a tiny mouth with pale lips. She wore no makeup, and looked young, even for a college student. Dez wondered if she was some wunderkind, the Doogie Howser of law students. The girl wore a chunky sweater of alternating blue and aqua horizontal stripes—as well as a judgmental look on her face.

Dez looked down. "Uh—no, not really."

"Not for any of your classes?"

"I usually get everything I need in the regular library," Dez said carefully.

"The *regular* library."

"Well, I'm not pre-law, or anything," Dez said, a note of protest in her voice.

"We have one of the most comprehensive law libraries in the state of California," the girl said condescendingly, "and you've spent nearly four years at this university without coming here?"

Dez had had enough. "Yes, despite your incredibly welcoming attitude. Hard to believe."

The girl scoffed. "Do you want me to help you with LexisNexis or not?"

"I do," Dez said. "That's why I came up to the desk. I wasn't looking for a lecture on my life choices."

Visibly rolling her eyes, the girl got up from her chair and walked Dez over to a bank of keyboards and monitors. After showing Dez the search functions and how to find the text from the results of the searches—the girl went so fast, Dez could barely keep up—she turned quickly and went back to the desk, where she immediately started arguing with another student who had walked up.

"Well, at least it's not just me," Dez muttered.

She typed in *Jennifer Morgenstern* at the search cursor.

The system thought for a few minutes, the cursor blinking in the top left corner. Dez knew these systems were much faster than doing all this work by hand, but it seemed a bit silly to just sit back and watch a blinking cursor. Zen and the Art of Legal Database Searches. She sighed and leaned back, wondering if she perhaps should have brought Exodus Nights.

After what seemed like hours—but, Dez saw by her watch, was less than ten minutes—the system kicked back four hundred and thirteen thousand instances. Dez swore at herself under her breath. She had let herself get unnerved by the law library assistant and forgot about the Boolean search. She typed *Jennifer AND Morgenstern*. She paused, and then for good measure—and remembering the girl had told her to hyphenate multiple-word location searches—typed AND *New-Hampshire*.

The system's screen again went black for a moment, with only the cursor blinking in the left-hand top corner. She hoped this wouldn't take as long as the first search. One minute turned into five, but finally the search was complete.

Five results came back. In the first four were cases, the *Jennifer* and the *Morgenstern* weren't the same person. The fifth one, however, was a bull's eye. Morgenstern v. Bethany, 1986. It was a civil case in Nashua, New Hampshire.

The plaintiff's filing was there for Dez to read—and she did. Jennifer Morgenstern was suing Frank Bethany and Showcase Monument Publishing for intellectual property theft. And it was exactly what Dez thought it might be—she accused Frank Bethany of stealing significant portions of her novel Murder on a Lifeboat for his book Exodus Nights. She claimed damages of over half a million dollars and wanted to be named as co-author and have a cut of the future proceeds of the book. Frank Bethany was represented by, as Dez figured out, a Showcase Monument Publishing lawyer.

The opening arguments had been given in the case, and there was a list of witnesses. Dez recognized a few of the names from the Dartmouth paper's editor box. But the first witness scheduled to appear—a man named Aaron Hawthorne—failed to do so. The judge had granted the plaintiff's request for a recess, and then, Dez read, the suit was withdrawn.

Just like that.

Dez didn't like the way that looked at all.

She did another search for Frank Bethany, in both New Hampshire and New York, where Showcase Monument was based. She found some references to Exodus Nights in a transcript from another case; she found a case in which another Dartmouth professor, suing a neighbor, had called Frank Bethany as a witness. But nothing useful. As far as Dez could tell, Frank Bethany made no other appearance in court in New Hampshire, and for that matter, neither did Jennifer Morgenstern.

Dez couldn't figure out what she wanted to do next. And she had no idea what to say to Frankie the next time she called.

Dez sat back and took everything in. Jennifer Morgenstern had been wronged by Frank Bethany—or at least thought she had been wronged—in New Hampshire five years before. Now she moved all the way across the country and was introducing herself as *the* Frank Bethany. Was there a method to Frankie's madness? And what was Frankie trying to get out of it? Stalking? Revenge?

Dez logged off the search system and walked past the dour white girl at the entrance, who said "You're welcome" pointedly as Dez exited. But Dez was too preoccupied to respond; it barely registered with her that the girl had said anything.

It was almost eleven, and instead of walking home in the damp, piercing January chill, she crossed over to the campus commons and got a cheap turkey sandwich and a Diet Coke from the deli. She sat by herself and listlessly flipped through one of her law enforcement textbooks.

What would Dez have done in that situation? Supposing Dez had written a crime novel that Dr. Gallows had stolen and rewritten, would she sue? If she sued and her first witness failed to show up, would she move to New York and introduce herself to her dates as Roberta Gallows?

She looked up when a ray of sun broke through the clouds and realized she had been there for over an hour. She finished up, cleared her table, and walked to her apartment. When she opened the front door, she saw Rhonda on the phone.

"Oh—she just walked in. Hang on." Rhonda handed the phone to Dez with a knowing look on her face. "Here you go, *Desirée*." Dez felt her heart speed up just a little bit.

"Hi, Desirée," Audrey said.

"Audrey!" Dez said, a little more enthusiastically than she had intended.

"Listen—I talked to the manager here, and he showed me how to put in a special order for that book you wanted. Um—*Murder on a Lifeboat*, right?"

"Right," Dez said. "Wow, you can do that?"

"Well, since it's officially out of print, we may not get a hit on it," Audrey said. "It was remaindered a while ago."

"Remaindered?"

"Oh, sorry, book nerd term. It means they're not selling well and publishers are getting rid of them at a big discount. It also means they can't be returned to the publisher, which means the chance that they'll have one in stock are small. But you never know. At least the request is in the system now, so if there *is* a copy returned, they can ship it out to you."

"Oh. All right, cool, I guess."

"Yeah, it's not great news, but it's better than nothing. And since it got remaindered, you might be able to find it at a random bookstore for a lot less. Maybe two or three dollars instead of sixteen or seventeen."

"Is it in paperback?"

"Nope, it didn't sell well enough for that. Just the hardback."

"Okay, well, thanks for letting me know." Dez looked over at Rhonda.

"Ask her out, fool," Rhonda said quietly.

"Can I—uh—can I thank you for going through all that trouble?" Dez said.

"Oh, I actually *love* tracking down books like this. I'm going to get it for you, just you wait."

"Well—" Dez paused, gathering herself up again. "I still think it's going above and beyond. Maybe I could take you to dinner tonight?"

"Sure!" Audrey said, brightly. "I'd love that. Is late okay? I get off at nine."

Dez tried to temper her enthusiasm; maybe Rhonda was wrong about her pessimism. "That's cool."

"Great! Maybe we can go to Jack and Jill's, that new diner down on Sixth Street in Long Beach. That's closer to my place, anyway."

"Oh—you live in Long Beach?"

"Yeah, right off Pine."

"I'm in Long Beach too. The student apartments off Bellflower."

They talked for another five minutes until Audrey said she had to get back to work—her break was over.

Dez hung up, giddy.

9

BY MARCH, DEZ THOUGHT OF FRANKIE—WHEN SHE thought of her at all—as "the crazy writer who got ripped off"—or, more often and more happily, as the reason Dez had met Audrey.

Dez and Audrey had fun together—and they were together all the time. She loved that Audrey smelled like books. She loved the feel of Audrey's hands, whether it was a gentle touch on her shoulder after dinner, or the passionate grip around Dez's wrists during their lovemaking. She was spontaneous, agreeing to drive up the California coast, just on a whim, when they both found themselves free from their restaurant and bookstore jobs one weekend in February. They had stayed in a cheap hotel in a little city in Dominguez County called Estancia, where they walked on the beach, ate at a cheap but delicious burger place, and Dez got a job application from the sheriff's office. That night, they got drunk on tequila a block from the hotel, and they walked back, giggling, Audrey's hands on Dez's hips. When they got to their room, Dez threw the door open, and Audrey spun Dez around, giving her a full, passionate kiss before they closed the door behind them.

Dez had often been the dominant one in her relationships, especially since moving to Long Beach. She always seemed to pick the shy, tentative, inexperienced ones. Frankie hadn't been the only girl Dez had broken in on the whole Sapphic thing.

That wasn't the case with Audrey, though. Audrey had been in relationships with women since she was sixteen years old. Like Frankie, Audrey was older than Dez, but unlike Frankie, she wasn't critical of Dez's education status, or her age. Likewise, Dez didn't criticize Audrey's job at the bookstore; she couldn't find any work relevant to her art history degree.

Rhonda had blown up at Dez one night in mid-March.

"Okay, I like Audrey and all," Rhonda said, "and she's clearly a better fit for you than Frankie, but you've seriously been with her every day for the last six weeks. It's like you went on your first date and they stitched you two together like some sort of Frankenstein horror movie."

Dez apologized, but in the back of her head, she was thinking about the feel of Audrey's lips on hers. She knew there was only six hours before the end of Audrey's shift at the bookstore and felt a pang of pain as she called Audrey to cancel to go with Rhonda to see some lawyer movie that starred Joe Pesci and the Karate Kid.

"Don't worry about it," Audrey said. "I understand. I've actually got a lead on your book."

"My book?"

"*Murder on ze Lifeboat*," Audrey said in a low voice, affecting a bad Russian accent. "My contacts have informed me of some *een*-teresting possibilities."

"Okay, Natasha," Dez said.

"Natasha? Should I call you Boris?"

"As long as you don't have moose and squirrel in bed with you when I stop by later, you can call me whatever you want."

But Dez didn't want Audrey to find *Murder on a Lifeboat* anymore. She hadn't thought about Frankie—or Jennifer Morgenstern—since that trip up the coast to Estancia. If Dez were in Audrey's position, she would have given up looking for that book weeks ago.

Dez's night at the movies with Rhonda was enjoyable. Rhonda opined frequently about Marisa Tomei's stunning good looks, while Dez couldn't get past her Brooklyn accent. Dez felt a twinge of sadness that her friendship with Rhonda was going on the backburner, but just the same, she kept pushing down the desire to look at her watch, counting down the minutes until the friendship night was over so she could go to Audrey's apartment.

The Saturday before Long Beach State's spring break dawned gray and surprisingly cold for April in Southern California. Dez had gotten used to thunderstorms growing up in Lake Charles, but after she moved, she barely saw one a year. Now the forecast called for thunderstorms that afternoon, and into the evening.

"Okay, missy," Dez said, spitting out the toothpaste while Audrey put on her makeup. "You said you had something planned for my birthday. You think it'll withstand this freakish weather?"

Audrey brushed her long, shiny black hair. "I might have to change the order we do stuff in during the day. I think the rain will hold off for a few hours. And I'll have to give you your present early."

"Oh hell no," Dez said, smiling. "How *dare* you ruin my birthday by giving me my birthday present a few hours before you wanted to."

Audrey reached out and touched Dez lightly and affectionately on the nose.

They were out of Audrey's apartment a few minutes later, and they walked south on Pine, toward the beach. Audrey carried one of her larger purses.

"Our first stop this beautiful, cool April morning will be Benedict and Company," Audrey said.

"Oh, fancy-schmancy," Dez said.

"Well, you're worth it," Audrey said, smiling.

At brunch, after they had both ordered the French toast, Audrey pulled out the large, heavy present from her purse.

"That's why you've been carrying that monster purse," Dez said.

"Yes. And that's why we're going home before we head to the beach. I thought we could try to relive our weekend in Estancia without actually driving all the way up there."

"The tequila bar and the after-party too?"

Audrey got a wicked look on her face. "Most *definitely* the after-party. I'm not sure I'd want to go to the tequila bar. That was a hangover I won't soon forget."

"That's cool. I liked the after-party better anyway."

"Okay." Audrey clapped three times and put her elbows on the table. "Enough talk. Open it up."

Dez smiled at Audrey and tore off the ribbon and the wrapping paper.

As Dez expected, it was a hardback novel. She was wondering if Audrey had gotten her the Michael Chabon she'd been hinting at. Or maybe the new Louise Erdrich.

Instead, it was a book she never expected to see: *Murder on a Lifeboat. A novel. Jennifer Morgenstern.*

She ran her hand over the cover. It was a picture of a life preserver with the word "Murder" on it, laid out as if the word had been printed on the preserver itself. And "on a Lifeboat" was in a script that belonged on a romance novel.

The cover showed a bit of wear, a slight discoloration on the corner. She turned the book over and saw where the original price sticker had been pulled off incompletely; the remnants of the white label, discolored by a few years of bookshelf dust, left its telltale signs.

"I found it," Audrey said proudly. "You would not *believe* what I had to do to get this damn book."

"Wow," Dez said, needing to sound impressed and surprised instead of anxious. She didn't want to bring up Jennifer Morgenstern or Frankie, and certainly didn't want to talk about the one-night stand that felt like a lifetime ago.

"I finally tracked it down at a used bookstore when I went up to Hollywood a couple of weeks ago," she said. "Two weeks ago, in fact. You know when that was?"

Dez nodded. It had been the night that Dez spent with Rhonda and Joe Pesci.

"And I thought it was fate, you know? You and I met because you were looking for that book. And I looked and looked, through the computer at the store, and I even looked at that used bookstore up the coast—do you remember how weird that place was?"

Dez nodded again. She barely remembered the unusual bookstore, but she did remember the tequila hangover.

"On pretty much the first night we spent away from each other since we started dating—there it was, like a beacon leading me back to you."

"I can't believe it," Dez said, and that was true enough.

She opened to the first chapter.

And there was the opening scene of *Exodus Nights*.

The grisliness of the murder was, if it was possible, even more graphic and violent and bloody than the Frank Bethany version. The names were different, the body of water was in a different part of the world, but it was definitely the same scene.

Dez flipped back a couple of pages and checked the copyright date: the year before *Exodus Nights* was released.

Frankie hadn't been telling the truth in a lot of ways, but in a sense she was telling all the truth in the world.

Dez felt her anxiety shift. Yes, there was still the lie-by-omission about that night with Frankie, but there was something else, and she couldn't put her finger on it. There were still red flags there, but Dez realized that there *was* a method to Frankie's madness. It had been there, staring her in the face, if she had just recognized the truth through the lens of Frankie's story.

Dez closed the book and smiled. "This is an incredible surprise," she said.

"Do you like it?"

Dez nodded. "I love it."

Audrey looked visibly relieved. "Thank *God*. I was afraid you'd forgotten about it. But once I found out that book existed, I just *had* to get it. Too weird that it's got so much connection to *Exodus Nights*, right?"

"Right." Dez grinned in spite of the gnawing unease. Audrey was prone to this kind of tenacity, but she combined it with a kindness, a gentleness, a sweetness, an empathy, which none of Dez's previous girlfriends and lovers—especially Frankie—exhibited at all.

"This is fantastic, Audrey," Dez said, completely overwhelmed by the thoughtfulness of the gesture and for the work it took for her to find it.

Then, in addition to the vague apprehension, Dez felt a pang of guilt. After her dinner with Audrey that first Friday night, Frankie had called and left a message on Dez's machine. Dez had meant to return it, but didn't know what she would say. It was the only call Frankie would make. Dez hadn't been back to Redondo Beach since, nor seen the woman who threw the party in Westwood. Although she was more Rhonda's friend anyway.

Audrey was still looking at Dez expectantly.

"What?"

"Speaking of *Exodus Nights*, did you see what *else* was in there?" Audrey's voice was excited; she was shaking her foot nervously.

Dez had turned to the first chapter, but hadn't seen the envelope tucked into the middle of the book. "What's this?" she said, determined to put a playful note in her voice. "Oh, it's like when my gramma would give me a book for Christmas with a five-dollar bill in it. You gave me five dollars?"

Audrey ignored the bad attempt at a joke, and almost squeaked with excitement. "I think you'll like it much more than a five-dollar bill."

Dez took the envelope; it wasn't sealed.

The two tickets inside were for that night.

An Evening with Frank Bethany. At the Los Angeles Arts Theater.

Dez looked up, puzzled. *"An Evening with Frank Bethany?"*

"Yes, can you believe it? He's promoting his new novel. I think he's on *Good Day L.A.* tomorrow morning, and he's being interviewed by that book reviewer on the NPR station."

Dez was speechless.

"I bet you didn't even know he was coming to town, did you?"

Dez shook her head. "I had absolutely no idea."

"He hasn't done a book tour in two years. L.A. is his only promotional appearance in the state!"

"He hasn't done a book tour in two years?"

"Nope. I heard something weird happened to him on his last tour, but the rumors among the literati are all over the place. Pregnant mistress, DUI, heroin overdose, stalker, you name it, it's a rumor."

"Stalker?"

Audrey looked at Dez. "It wasn't *you*, was it?" Then she laughed.

The anxiety in Dez's stomach took shape. Jennifer Morgenstern was in Los Angeles, a recent transplant from New Hampshire, after having her book stolen. And she wasn't over it; far from it.

"Don't you want to know how I scored those tickets?" Audrey prodded.

Dez looked up. "What? Oh—these were hard to get?"

"Tougher than the Lakers courtside."

"Wow. How did you manage it?"

The Russian accent was back. "Oh, darlink, I have my connections," Audrey cooed.

"Oh, fine, Natasha, don't tell me. It's almost like you don't want to get as good of a gift for *your* birthday."

Audrey laughed.

Dez laughed with her, but the dread in the pit of her stomach made her feel nauseated. Those few days she had spent with *Exodus Nights* and with Frankie represented a strange, surreal time for her. She remembered how restless she had been, how strong her thirst was to figure out what was going on. She remembered the discussion with Dr. Gallows, she remembered how Rhonda had to talk her off the ledge so that she could get her brain concentrating on something besides Frankie. And Audrey—beautiful, grounded, sane Audrey—had gotten her brain to break the vacuum seal of the Frankie mystery. And now, with the theft still raw and the thief in town, Dez worried that this book tour might be why Frankie had moved to Los Angeles.

"Do you know how long Frank Bethany is in town?" Dez asked, as casually as she could.

Audrey narrowed her eyes. "Not really. Maybe a few days. Why?"

"Just curious."

"You don't like the tickets?"

Dez realized her smile had faltered. "No, no, I *love* the tickets!" she said, her voice sounding as enthusiastic as she could make it. "It's just such a mind trip! I can't wrap my head around the fact that you got these tickets. I mean, they're so impossible to get."

The effervescent brunette server came with their food. Dez pulled the wrapping paper out of the way. "Oh, is it somebody's birthday?" the server said brightly.

"That would be Desirée," Audrey giggled.

"Desirée, happy birthday," the server said.

"It's her fiftieth birthday today," Audrey said. "Doesn't she look *wonderful*?"

The server looked at Dez, half-questioning, half-shocked.

"Don't listen to her," Dez said. "I'm twenty-two."

"Doing anything exciting tonight?"

"We're going to see one of her favorite authors do a reading," Audrey said. "Well, I assume it's a reading. There's a new book out."

"Oh! Which author?"

"You heard of Frank Bethany?"

"Does he write romance?"

Audrey smiled. "Afraid not."

"I'm strictly a romance reader. I thought it might be Nora Roberts or Danielle Steel someone like that." The server put her hands on her hips. "You two need anything else right now?"

Dez shook her head.

"All right, holler if you need anything." She turned and was gone.

Dez looked at her plate of French toast, and the little plastic syrup pitcher balanced next to the sphere of butter. She remembered the criminal evidence class she had taken the year before, when they did the unit on blood evidence. She had to memorize a chart on coagulation. She looked at the syrup again, then picked the pitcher up and set it off the plate. Cutting a corner off the French toast, she forced herself to put it in her mouth and chew it. It was delicious, and still it could barely go down.

Dez looked across the table. Audrey was beaming.

10

THEY WALKED BACK TO AUDREY'S APARTMENT. HALFWAY there, Audrey took Dez's hand. Dez felt herself tense up.

"Don't worry about it, Dez," Audrey breathed. "To everyone else, we're just two college girls. We're friends, having a good time on a Saturday morning. Straight girls hold hands all the time. No one has any idea that we're going back to my apartment to have fantastic sex."

Dez smiled and took a deep breath.

Dez was used to talking to her girlfriends the way Audrey was talking to her. Her girlfriends in the past had been giggly, tentative, raw. For many of them, if they had kissed other girls it had been under the pretense of making their boyfriends jealous—or horny. Her previous girlfriends were used to fantasizing about other women when their boyfriends were on top of them.

Dez told herself she was just being paranoid about the author reading. Nothing was going to happen; it was just her criminal justice classes putting crazy thoughts in her head.

And besides, it was her birthday, and there was a beautiful woman walking next to her, holding her hand, and she wanted to enjoy the rest of the day.

Audrey took her keys out before her front door was in view, and unlocked the door quickly, smoothly, with none of the nervousness that Dez was trying to quell. She unbuttoned Dez's shirt before they were halfway across the living room and Dez soon found herself face down on the bed, Audrey on top of her, biting her ear, her hand between Dez's legs. She lost herself.

Afterward, they held each other, Dez snuggling into the crook of Audrey's shoulder, still trying to catch her breath.

"So are you excited for the reading?" Audrey said.

"Not nearly as excited as I was a few minutes ago," Dez said.

"I think we should get dressed up tonight," Audrey said. "I think we should put on evening dresses and makeup and pretend we're ingénues."

Dez laughed. "Oh, honey, you can do that, maybe, but I haven't had a dress on since I moved to California."

"Why not?" Audrey said. "You've got fantastic legs. You should show them off."

"I pretended to be all girly-girl in front of my mom for too long. I don't need my girlfriend—my *girlfriend*, of all people—telling me I need to dress more like a girly-girl."

"Not because I want you to be girly," Audrey said. "Because I want to dress up with you."

"Maybe I should go in a tux," Dez said.

"Do you have a tux?"

Dez paused. "No."

"Maybe a suit and tie?"

"No," Dez admitted. "I don't know how to tie a tie anyway."

"You've got a little black dress, though, right? I know, I've seen it in your closet."

"Hah. There's something in my closet, for sure."

"The irony is killing me," Audrey deadpanned. "So, when you go back to your place to get ready, you can put on that little black dress, and you can show off your fantastic legs, and your runner's butt, and I'll come pick you up in that black-and-red floral dress that you like so much, and we can go be debutantes at the Frank Bethany ball."

Dez pictured Audrey in the floral dress and felt her defenses weaken, but still protested. "I don't even know if that little black dress fits anymore."

Audrey scoffed. "You're still wearing those tight jeans that you owned when you were sixteen. Of course that little black dress will still fit you."

They both got out of bed and lazily started to get dressed.

Dez looked out the window. The rain had started again.

"It just started to rain," Dez said. "Guess we're not going to be doing the walk on the beach today."

"That's okay," Audrey said. "What we just did was pretty good too."

Dez smiled. "So what do you want to do instead?"

"Oh, don't you worry about that."

Audrey had a 1985 Toyota Corolla that was parked around the corner on Pine and Seventh. Dez tried not to get her book too wet on the way to the car. The tickets were tucked safely inside the front bookflap.

They drove a few blocks to Ocean Boulevard, then crossed over the Los Angeles River to the Seaside Freeway. The traffic was stop-and-go most of the way.

"Start reading the book to me, Desirée," Audrey said.

"Oh, no," Dez said. "It's super violent and kind of messed up. Definitely not driving material."

She thought about telling Audrey, right then and there, about Frankie and Frank Bethany and Jennifer Morgenstern and the plagiarism and her misgivings about the evening. She opened her mouth but didn't know where to begin. And then the moment passed.

"If you want music," Audrey said, "all I've got in the car is Indigo Girls and that new Nirvana album."

"You can't even bring yourself to throw a little Madonna in with that? For listening to depressing music, you sure are an upbeat person."

"I get all the negative feelings out when I'm listening to music so I'm not a bitch when I talk to real people," Audrey said, then stuck her tongue out at Dez.

"Don't be sticking that out at me unless you intend to use it," Dez said.

Audrey shot her a dirty look.

The freeway crossed the Vincent Thomas bridge and Audrey got over to exit the freeway. They passed a sign that said, "Cruise Ships — Next Exit."

"Oh, my word, you're taking me on a cruise!" Dez said. "A cruise for spring break! My friends will be so jealous."

Audrey giggled. "Not on my salary, I'm not."

They drove past the harbor, past 22nd Street Park, and pulled into a parking lot near the Cabrillo Marina.

"Are we going where I think we're going?" Dez said.

Audrey pulled into a parking space. "If you think we're going to the aquarium, then yes."

Dez playfully slapped Audrey's shoulder. "How did you know I love this aquarium?"

"Uh, because I pay attention, Desirée. You practically broadcast it whenever any marine-related subject comes up. Jellyfish. Manta rays. Dolphin-safe tuna."

"You know I've worked here as a docent in the summers."

"No," Audrey said, in a mocking tone. "I have absolutely never heard any of the hundreds of stories about you working here in the summers. I also didn't hear any of the carefully crafted tales about the trouble you had with the colony of blue-banded gobies."

Dez elbowed Audrey. "*School* of blue-banded gobies, Audrey. Get it right."

Once they had purchased their tickets and were inside, Dez turned into a tour guide. The aquarium was small, but Dez was inspired by the Frank Gehry-designed building. "I like to start at the open ocean exhibit and work backwards," Dez said.

"You're such a rebel."

"I know. Look, here's the fish diversity tank."

"Fish diversity tank. It's like a metaphor for our relationship," Audrey teased. "I think Jesse Jackson would be incredibly inspired by us."

"Yeah," Dez said, "a true rainbow trout coalition."

Audrey rolled her eyes.

Dez led them through most of the exhibits, spending a few minutes talking about the basking sharks. Audrey pretended to be interested in the facts as Dez presented them. Did you know basking sharks are the second largest fish in the world? Many people are frightened of basking sharks, but they don't eat surfers; they're filter-feeders, eating only plankton and fish eggs. Basking sharks are slow, swimming no faster than three miles per hour.

"Fascinating," said Audrey.

They turned the corner to the mudflats. "I think the mudflats are my favorite part of the aquarium," Dez said, a little moonily. "I like the worlds colliding, where the birds meet the fish, where the animals live in both the water and the sand. It makes me kind of wish for that kind of life."

"You think you'll always live by the ocean?" asked Audrey.

Dez shrugged. "I don't know. My favorite place when I was growing up was going by the riverbank. You ever heard of the Calcasieu River?"

"The what?"

"Never mind, it's not an important river or anything. It's just the main river in Lake Charles. And there are a million little fingers of the Calcasieu. It's kind of like the mudflats. Water birds and crawfish and these little fish. Thousands and thousands of these little sunfish, some of them only six inches long. We had a riverbank just down maybe a thousand yards from our house. When I got out of school for the summer, I'd go down there with my fishing pole and some tackle and find a nice quiet secluded place." Dez watched an orange-pink bird land and clean itself with its long, slightly upturned bill. "I had an older brother who wasn't very nice to me. But he didn't like the water."

"Afraid of alligators?"

Dez scoffed. "Y'all think gators are everywhere in Louisiana."

"You don't have alligators in Lake Charles?"

Dez paused sheepishly. "Uh, I guess we do, but *I* never saw any on my part of the river. No, one of his friends just wouldn't leave him alone one day. I don't know, it's like he was hell-bent on making my brother's life miserable that day. Well, this jackass friend of his tackled him when he was standing on the riverbank, and they both fell in. I guess my brother was eight or nine. Anyway, my brother smacked his face on a stump sticking out of the water. Broke his nose. Kinda lucky that was all. The other kid got his foot all tangled up in some roots and cut his leg open pretty badly. My brother's hated the river ever since. But I loved it—I actually think part of me loved it *because* he hated it. I made sure nobody knew where I was pretty much the whole summer."

"Your mom didn't care?"

"Not when I came home with dinner," Dez said. "I'd catch crawfish if the fish weren't biting. But they usually were biting pretty good. I got a twenty-pound catfish one day. I must have been thirteen or fourteen. I think that was just before I started high school."

"You know your cute little Louisiana drawl has gotten way more pronounced since you've been talking." Audrey rubbed Dez on the arm. "Kind of like how you get when you talk to your mamma on the phone."

"Mamma says I'm starting to talk like I'm putting on airs," Dez said.

"I guess. Not that I think that's a bad thing."

Dez decided not to ruin this day by telling Audrey about Frankie. Dez promised herself she'd bring it up tomorrow. After they woke up, maybe after breakfast. It would be better to tell Audrey without the anxiety that Frankie would do something at the author event that night. They'd probably even laugh about it.

They swung around to the kelp forest area, then through the doors to the outdoor touch pool. The rain was coming down harder now, but the covered touch pool area was crowded. Dez wasn't keen on touching the starfish or the other species and hated the over-enthusiastic little kids going crazy to try to get their hands on the wildlife.

"I tell you, if I ever end up in hell," Dez said, "I'll get turned into a starfish in one of these damn touch pools. Little kids with their grubby mitts eating McDonald's and picking their noses and then sticking their hands in the water. Ugh."

"I swear," Audrey said, a deadly serious note in her voice, looking deep into Dez's eyes, "that I will never eat McDonald's and then pick my nose and stick my hands on you."

Dez laughed. "Can't beat that with a stick."

They walked laughing in the rain, without an umbrella, back to the Corolla. They listed the best things about Los Angeles that they still hadn't experienced and planned to do together: Dez had yet to eat fried chicken at Knott's Berry Farm; Audrey had never been to Venice Beach. Neither of them had ever been to the Los Angeles Arts Theater before, even though it was built in the twenties and was supposed to have been the location where Elizabeth Taylor's first movie was released.

The traffic was horrible on the way back to Dez's apartment off Bellflower, but Audrey was in a good mood, and so was Dez, and even got Dez to sing along to an Indigo Girls song.

"You need to get some Aretha," Dez sniffed. "Jesse Jackson wouldn't like it that you don't have any Aretha CDs. This whiny white people music is going to give me a damn complex."

Audrey pulled up next to the curb in front of Dez's apartment. Dez looked around briefly, and seeing no one, pecked Audrey on the lips. "That wasn't a real kiss," Audrey pouted.

"You'll get a real kiss after the show tonight," Dez said, opening the door and getting out of the car. "In my little black dress and everything." She closed the door behind her as Audrey blew her a kiss and waved goodbye.

Dez felt light as she walked to the apartment—and then realized she had left the book in the car. She sighed—she'd thought she might read some more of it before she figured out her dress, makeup, and hair for the evening. "Such a pain in the ass," she said to herself. "If I wanted to get all dressed up for a date, I'd date a stupid boy." But she was smiling to herself to think of her and Audrey together, dressed up in girly dresses, turning heads with Audrey's curves and Dez's runner's body.

She called Rhonda's name when she got into the apartment, but there was no answer. She went upstairs; Rhonda's bedroom door was open, but it was empty.

Dez wrapped her hair for a shower, then thought of using the fancy body wash her mother had sent her for Christmas. It took some digging under the counter before she found it. After her shower, she pulled out a shoe box from her top shelf and found some perfume— a bit of Carolina Herrera from a sample that had been forced on her at Emporium.

The little black dress was a Paquette, and it still fit her well, if a little snugly across the rear, but she hadn't been nearly as strong a runner when she had bought the dress, and she knew the extra inch around her hips was muscle. She admired herself in the mirror and, just for a moment, saw herself the way Audrey saw her—and maybe even the way Frankie had seen her three months before.

She had a pair of low heels—her only pair of heels, in spite of her mother's horror about it—and they were, to Dez's relief, black and shiny and perfect with the dress.

She had expected to be a little disgusted with the way she looked, or at the very least, not recognize herself in the mirror. But she was pleasantly surprised to find that the dress looked good on her, accentuating all the things she liked about her body, even if the femininity the dress exuded was a little much.

"Damn," Dez said, "I don't really look like me, but I guess I look pretty good."

She looked at the clock; Audrey was going to pick her up in about thirty minutes. She heard the front door open and close, and Rhonda called her name.

"Up here!" Dez called out, and she picked up a black-and-white zebra-striped purse—the most formal purse she had—and went downstairs.

Rhonda was sitting on the sofa, holding the remote control, about to turn the television on. When she saw Dez, she burst into laughter. Dez was mortified.

"Dez," she said, tears of mirth starting to stream down her cheeks, "what in the *hell* are you wearing?"

"I'm wearing a black dress," Dez offered lamely.

"Who are you and what have you done with Dez?" Rhonda hooted.

"Don't be an asshole," Dez snapped. "You know I look damn fine in this. I look a lot better than most of the party girls you bring home."

"Oh, take it easy, Dez," Rhonda said, bringing her gales of laughter under control. "I just didn't expect to have Naomi Campbell walking down the staircase in my house."

"Please. You call me Naomi Campbell and now I'm supposed to forgive you."

"Now, don't take this the wrong way, but that dress was Audrey's idea, wasn't it?"

"So what if it was?"

"I'm just saying, Dez, that it's fine that you've disappeared up her butt for the last two months. You've been single for a while, you deserve some great sex, some good relationship karma, some blah blah blah. But just remember, your friends have been there for you for a long time, so don't just cut us loose."

Dez paused. "Yeah, okay, Rhonda."

"Okay." Rhonda paused. "And you do look really good in that dress. Your ass looks fantastic."

"Ugh," Dez said. "You went into creepy territory with that."

"Not saying I wanna bang you or anything. Just saying your ass looks good."

Dez put up a hand to stop her. "Okay, thank you, appreciate the compliment, don't say it again."

Rhonda laughed. "It's really a fine line to walk with you, Dez. Can't laugh at the way you look, can't perv on you."

"What? *Perv* on me?"

Rhonda nodded. "The girl who was here Friday night. And Saturday morning. She's from England. She's teaching me some new phrases. Some of them are dumb, like saying *pants* when you mean *underwear*, but I like 'perving on you.' It's delicious and naughty."

"Okay, creepy chick," Dez said. "Audrey's going to pick me up soon. Don't go, uh, *perving* on her either."

Dez walked into the downstairs bathroom and checked her makeup one more time.

"So why are you all dressed up?" Rhonda said. "What are you up to—is it the opera? The ballet?"

"Audrey got us tickets to an author reading tonight."

"An author reading? Barf." Rhonda shook her head. "A concert or a Lakers game I could see. An *author* reading? Man, unless it's that crazy violent wolf-insect-sex author you were into a few months ago—"

Rhonda looked at Dez's face.

"Oh my God! It *is* him! That writer my brother likes. You were asking about that book when you met Audrey and now she bought you tickets to it!" Rhonda cackled. "That is just *too* rich. Did you ever talk to her about—uh—what was her name? That girl you danced with at the party in Westwood? The one who had you convinced that she wrote that weird book? The one you were totally into for about a week?"

"Frankie."

"Yeah!" Rhonda smacked her knee for emphasis. "That was it. Did you ever talk about her?"

Dez shrugged. "Nope. Didn't really see a need to."

"Did you ever see her again after that one date?"

"No. She called me once and left a message, but that was it." Dez felt a twinge of guilt.

"Hah." Rhonda smirked. "Did she go back to disappointing *men* in bed?"

"Oh, come on, now," Dez said. "That girl had problems."

"Problems in bed," Rhonda said. "And usually girls that crazy are *dynamite*."

Dez paused. "You know, I think that Frank Bethany really *did* steal that book from her."

"Really? She wasn't just a narcissist looking for attention?"

Dez laughed. "Well, I think she was a narcissist looking for attention, but that doesn't mean she didn't get her book stolen."

They were silent for a while.

"Rhonda, this is going to sound crazy, but part of me thinks Frankie's going to show up at that author reading tonight."

Rhonda's face was blank.

"I mean," Dez clarified, "show up and *do something*. Like, I don't know, make a scene, try to rush the stage, maybe. Expose his plagiarism to the world."

"You really think she would do that?"

"I don't know. Just—she told me *she* was Frank Bethany, which is crazy enough, but then I find out that he stopped touring for his new releases and it was maybe because of a stalker."

"Maybe because of a stalker?" Rhonda's skeptical tone made Dez feel foolish.

"I'm just thinking—why would she lie about who she is if she *wasn't* planning on confronting him when he's in L.A.?"

"Uh," Rhonda said, "if she pretended to be him, doesn't that just draw attention to herself? Like, if I were going to make a scene at some celebrity event, I'd be the most unassuming, quiet-as-a-mouse person you've ever seen—so no one would suspect me."

Dez smirked. "Like you could be unassuming if you tried."

Rhonda shrugged. "You don't know that. I got a little crush on Marisa Tomei. Maybe I'll be her quiet little accent coach for her next movie. Teach her how to roll her R's."

"This isn't a random celebrity crush, Rhonda. She used to be his student at Dartmouth."

Rhonda crossed her arms. "Okay, I see that you're intent on talking yourself into this. So what do you want to do about it, Mrs. Fletcher? You gonna call the police and tell them that some girl you banged once, who lied about her name, might sorta kinda possibly maybe do something like jump up on stage and tell people he stole her book? Is there anything even illegal about that?"

"Maybe she'll try to hurt him."

Rhonda scoffed. "The cops would tell you to go back to Cabot Cove."

Dez tapped her foot. "You're probably right. Okay—when Audrey gets here, don't breathe a *word* of what I just said. We're going to have a nice, romantic evening, and we don't need it ruined by my paranoia."

Rhonda laughed. "It'd serve you right. Not telling Audrey she got you tickets to see the guy your ex-lover pretended to be."

"It's complicated. I wouldn't even know where to start."

There was a knock at the door. Dez shot Rhonda a sharp look. Rhonda mimed zipping her lips.

Dez opened the door. Audrey was there, resplendent in a red-and-black floral dress. She had on a little more makeup than usual.

"Holy shit, Dez, you look *hot*," Audrey said. "That dress looks incredible on you."

"You look pretty great yourself."

"You don't even look like dykes," Rhonda offered from the couch.

"I know," Dez said. "We look more like those bi-curious sorority girls you bring home."

"Oh, Dez, be nice," Audrey said. "Have you had a good birthday so far?"

"Oh, shit," Rhonda said. "It's your birthday."

"Don't worry about it," Dez said.

"It's your birthday and I totally forgot," said Rhonda. "Why didn't you remind me?"

"It's not a big deal." Dez shrugged. "After twenty-one, birthdays don't mean much anymore."

"At twenty-five, you can rent a car," Audrey offered.

"Woo hoo," Dez said. "Come on, let's get going, or parking's going to be a nightmare."

"Wait," Audrey said. "Aren't you going to take *Exodus Nights*?"

"I don't know," Dez said. "It's a paperback. Aren't you supposed to take your hardcovers to sign?"

"He'll be honored that you bought the book, period," Audrey said. "Go up and get it."

Dez walked up the stairs to get the book, and felt Audrey's eyes on her dress the whole time, drinking her in. She put a little more side-to-side in her hips and immediately felt ridiculous, but when she got to the top of the stairs she turned her head to look at Audrey. The look on Audrey's face made her feel a lot less ridiculous.

She took her copy of *Exodus Nights* from her dresser and walked back downstairs.

11

DEZ AND AUDREY GOT OUT OF THE COROLLA SEVERAL blocks away from the Los Angeles Arts Theater. Parking, as Dez had suggested, was a nightmare—and traffic hadn't been a treat either. Not only was there no street parking around the theater, but the two parking garages that Audrey was going to use as backup were both full. As they drove down San Vicente Boulevard, they saw a Yugo pull out from a parking place into traffic in front of them, and Audrey did a masterful job parallel parking into the tiny space.

"Almost as good as me," Dez said.

"My looks, or my parking job?"

Dez laughed, picking up *Exodus Nights*.

They got out and started walking.

"You have the tickets?" Audrey asked after half a block.

"The tickets? Oh, shit, no."

"Are they still in the book?"

Dez closed her eyes and remembered putting the ticket envelope inside the front flap. "Yes."

"Okay." Audrey's eyes met Dez's, and the anxiety must have been obvious. "Don't worry about it, babe. You left the book in my car earlier. I put it in a bag in the back seat."

They went back to the Corolla and Audrey pulled *Murder on a Lifeboat* out of the bag and handed it to Dez and locked up the car again. Sure enough, the tickets were tucked inside the front flap.

"Come on," Audrey said. "It starts in fifteen minutes."

They walked past a laundromat and a Del Taco, then cut through a small park to cross Wilshire. Dez thought about taking Audrey's hand, but she looked around; there were lots of dressed-up older people, possibly on their way to the same theater, and she didn't feel comfortable announcing their relationship.

She looked at Audrey and marveled at how this woman could have so quickly transformed her heart. She hadn't been in a dress in a long time—not since moving to Long Beach three and a half years before— and she couldn't believe that she had gotten dressed up in a girly-girl, figure-hugging little black dress for her lover.

And she also couldn't believe that Audrey would fall for a girl like her. Dez definitely liked more feminine, curvy girls like Audrey—and Frankie—but they didn't always go for her; she tended to be more butch in her dress and in her mannerisms. And while she liked California, California didn't always like her: Mettie, for one, had made fun of the way she talked, and Dez still couldn't get the Louisiana drawl out of her voice. She saw the way some people looked down on her the times that she said "y'all."

But there wasn't any of that second-guessing herself when it came to being with Audrey. Yes, Audrey liked books and the whole book culture thing way more than Dez did, and Audrey still called her "Desirée"—which was Dez's own fault for introducing herself as such when they first met—but she'd never been more comfortable in a relationship. She looked down at the two books in her hand and with a palpable sense of relief realized that she had dodged a bullet with Frankie. Frankie hadn't been interested in anything about Dez. She criticized the Cabrillo Aquarium, she criticized Dez for still being a student, she made Dez feel bad for wanting to eat the cheesecake point first. But none of that was an issue with Audrey; they could talk for hours, and they could both participate in the conversation, and Dez could express her feelings and tell her about her past and Audrey listened. Dez was a pessimist, but she felt her heart swell.

They got to the entrance of the theater. Dez looked at her watch. It was twenty minutes past seven.

"We have a few minutes," Dez said. "They never start on time, anyway. Do you want to go grab something quick at that Del Taco we passed? You haven't eaten since brunch, right?"

Audrey smiled. "And miss out on your birthday dinner later? Not a chance."

"Oh, come on, Audrey," Dez said crossly, although a smile was playing at the corners of her mouth. "Your birthday is going to come along and I'm definitely not going to be able to top this. Certainly not on a scholarship student's finances."

"It's my pleasure." Audrey held the door open for Dez. "We can figure other stuff out when it's my birthday. Maybe stuff that doesn't cost money." She flashed an evil and knowing grin at Dez. Dez smiled back at Audrey; she was so forward. Dez liked it.

They found their seats, and Audrey went out to go to the bathroom. Dez sat; the chair folded down, and the upholstered seat looked more comfortable than it was.

She looked around the hall, scanning for Frankie's face. She knew she was being paranoid, but she couldn't help herself. If Dez were in Frankie's shoes and wanted to make a scene, she'd arrive early, stake out a good spot, watch for patterns in the ushers' movements, making sure she could avoid any and all obstacles on the way to the stage. Dez was suddenly struck by the thought of what she would do if Frankie *did* rush the stage and accuse Frank Bethany of plagiarism. Would Dez stand up, holding *Murder on a Lifeboat* above her head, and shout, "It's true! He's a thief! Here's the book he stole!"

Dez noted with relief that no one in the hall resembled Frankie.

She opened *Murder on a Lifeboat* and began to read again.

The scene with the old man and the transforming couple was there, too, just as it was in *Exodus Nights*. The transformation was different, however; these weren't wolves transforming into insects, but rather people transforming into vampires. Dez thought she saw some parallels in the text with Anne Rice, although a quick check of the publication date made her realize that Jennifer Morgenstern might have only been able to reference *Interview with the Vampire*, and not even *The Vampire Lestat*. It was less interesting than Frank Bethany's work, but it was inarguably close enough to have been stolen.

Dez shook her head as the seats around her started to fill. The audacity of a professor to steal his student's work and publish it as his own—especially when the book in question had already been published. But audacious wasn't an adequate word for it—it was mindbogglingly stupid. It was stupid, first and foremost, because Jennifer Morgenstern wasn't an idiot. The publishing house that Jennifer had sold her book to wasn't under a Dartmouth professor's thumb—at least, Dez couldn't imagine a scenario in which that would be true. And the civil suit had been filed, but, she remembered from her LexisNexis research, it wasn't Jennifer's publishing company representing her, it was Jennifer herself named as the plaintiff. That seemed odd, too. And then, after a witness hadn't shown up, the lawsuit had been pulled, and *Exodus Nights* had continued to be published.

She flipped around in *Murder on a Lifeboat* until she came to the acknowledgments page. Jennifer Morgenstern thanked many people, starting with her editor, and a broad brushstroke of "The English and Journalism Department Staffs at Dartmouth University," and the last paragraph: "And to Aaron, for believing so strongly in me and my work. I love you."

Aaron.

Dez wondered if that referred to Aaron Hawthorne, the witness who hadn't shown up. And Dez wondered about what had happened. Right after Jennifer's boyfriend—the one who had believed so strongly in her—hadn't shown up to the civil trial, the lawsuit had been pulled. What had Aaron known? Why didn't he testify?

Dez flipped back to the beginning of the book and looked at the title page. Hancock-Noel Publishing, Boston. Not one of the big names, Dez thought. Not even big enough to have a New York office.

Audrey came over and sat down next to Dez. "You excited?"

"You bet," Dez said.

Dez craned her neck, looking around the hall at the new faces coming in. She might have missed Frankie, or Frankie might be in some sort of disguise. Dez wondered, briefly, if Frankie had legally changed her name from Jennifer Morgenstern in the last few months, or if she had gotten so wrapped up in the idea of revenge that she only saw herself as Frankie.

Not seeing Frankie in the crowd, Dez told herself that Frankie was probably just trying out an idea on a cute girl she met at a party.

Dez opened *Murder on a Lifeboat* at random. The book opened at "Chapter Thirteen." She read the first line on the left-hand page.

James took a long, slow drink of whiskey, looking at Pamela through the bottom of the glass.

She closed the book and pulled *Exodus Nights* out. She found the start of "Chapter 13" and read the first line.

He took a slow, deliberate sip of coffee, appraising her, her long lashes, her smoldering eyes, over the top of the white porcelain mug.

Dez almost laughed out loud. Yes. This was so obvious, and yet it was unprovable. So many names had changed. So many items were swapped out for other items. So many vampires were now insects and wolves; so many whiskey glasses were now coffee cups.

When Dez worked at the aquarium the previous summer before, she had a co-worker, Marv, who never did his assigned tasks. He spent hours figuring out ways that he could look like he had actually fed the kelpfish or had cleaned the handrails. Marv devised a system of tricking his co-workers into covering for him. But Dez quickly saw that Marv spent more time *avoiding* work than if he had done the work in the first place. She bit her tongue for two weeks, but finally couldn't stand it and told him so. He gave her the finger and walked away.

Dez wondered how hard Frank Bethany had to work to make it look like he hadn't stolen Frankie's work—or

Jennifer Morgenstern's work, as she corrected herself. She wondered if his other books had been thieved as well, or if he realized that writing his own stuff would actually be less work—and far less risk. She wished she were in front of the LexisNexis computer to figure more of this out.

But she tried to snap herself back to the present. She was with Audrey, a woman who worked hard to give her unique, thoughtful presents. She looked up, and realized Audrey was looking at her.

"Hey."

"Hey," Audrey said. "You went somewhere miles away just now."

"Yeah," Dez said. "I was just thinking about my birthday gifts. I, uh." She cleared her throat. "I actually asked about this book because I went on a date with the author."

Audrey stared at Dez.

"Before I started seeing you," Dez continued, the words coming out in a rush. "I went on a date with Fr—with Jennifer Morgenstern. Only she told me she wrote all of Frank Bethany's books."

Audrey blinked. "What?"

"It was a crazy date. This woman was kind of nuts. She had me convinced that she used Frank Bethany as a pen name." Dez laughed awkwardly. "She even told me her name was Frankie, not Jennifer Morgenstern."

Audrey narrowed her eyes. "Is this one of your weird jokes that I don't get?"

"I have weird jokes you don't get?"

Audrey nodded. "Is this one of them?"

The lights flickered on and off three times.

"Um, no," Dez said.

Audrey's brow furrowed and her voice had an edge. "Why the hell would you tell me about this now? I tried to find that book for *three months*—and it turns out that you *fucked* the author?"

"I—I don't know," Dez stammered. She hadn't heard Audrey swear like that before—it was sharp and harsh and caught her off guard. Some people hurried to their seats, others took their time. The lights started to dim.

"I thought we were bonding over *Murder on a Lifeboat*. And you were only interested in it because you were having sex with the woman who wrote it?"

"You and I *were* bonding," Dez whispered as the crowd noise died down.

"But you were still hung up on her."

"I—I wasn't hung up on her."

Dez looked in Audrey's face in the darkness. Her eyes were wide, then she blinked and crossed her arms. "How long before you and I started dating did you sleep with her?"

Dez winced.

Audrey shook her head and sat back.

There was applause as the curtain opened. Dez sat back and turned her attention to the stage.

Two comfortable-looking brown leather chairs stood on the stage, with a small table off to the side of each, and just as the curtains opened all the way, a woman Dez didn't recognize came out and the applause gathered steam.

"Good evening, everyone," she said, and then repeated herself as the applause finally died down. "You know me as Rebecca Fulton from City of Angels Public Radio." She was thin and had a mass of large, auburn hair. Dressed in a modest, long-sleeved black dress that ended just below her knees, with black ballet flats, she was riding the line between professional and casual.

Dez was wondering if Fulton was going to be interviewing Frank Bethany. First, however, she ran through a litany of housekeeping items, and then a call for pledges to the local public radio stations, trying to guilt the audience into opening their wallets. People were still filtering in, finding their seats with ushers' flashlights, so Dez supposed it was a decent enough transition into the real meat of the performance. Dez's attention had started to wander when Fulton finally said, "...so without further ado, here he is, PEN/Faulkner finalist and bestselling author—Frank Bethany!"

The applause was thunderous, like he was a rock star coming out on stage with a guitar thrown carelessly over his shoulder, rather than an author coming out with a smartly appointed tweed sports coat with elbow patches. He grinned sheepishly—and Dez thought, a little falsely modest—before bowing deeply to the audience in front of him, and then turning to both the left and the right and bowing deeply to them as well. Dez looked at Audrey, who was looking at her. The look on Audrey's face was one of both incredulity and anger, and Dez didn't blame her. Dez thought that the man they had paid to see was a cheat and a liar and probably a narcissistic jackass, and Dez wondered how different she herself was than him.

Dez turned back to look at Frank Bethany on stage. She shook her head. She couldn't believe what Bethany had put Frankie through.

She couldn't believe she'd told Audrey just before the lights went down.

Rebecca Fulton lobbed nothing but softballs at Frank Bethany, from a couple of easy setup questions about his childhood to his career teaching at Dartmouth. His childhood had nothing of substance in it, nothing to suggest that diabolical violence would be a differentiating feature of his work forty years later. His career as a professor started at SUNY Binghamton after he received his Ph.D. in English Literature. That led to a discussion of who Bethany's favorite writers were. They were all dead white men: Ernest Hemingway, Raymond Carver, Joseph Conrad. And William Shakespeare, of course—and Fulton smiled knowingly before comparing *Friendly Fire* to *Hamlet*. All the dead white men were staples of literature syllabi across the country, but not an edgy or even a vaguely interesting choice in the bunch. It made Dez wonder if Frank Bethany had had an original thought in his life.

The conversation shifted to Bethany's new novel, which had been released just two weeks before. When Rebecca Fulton said *The Apex and the Mountain Lion* had been launched at the end of March, Dez felt Audrey tense up next to her. She wasn't sure if it was because Audrey realized that Dez hadn't mentioned Frank Bethany's new book and therefore might not have been as into Frank Bethany's novels and she had believed. Dez was sorry both that she hadn't said anything sooner and that she had said anything at all. She reached over and took Audrey's hand in hers, in the anonymizing darkness, and gave it a squeeze. Audrey didn't squeeze back, but didn't pull her hand away either.

The novel, Bethany said, was about more than just survival, more than just solitude. It was more than just a story about man versus nature, human versus apex predator, human versus apex of the mountain. It was a story that explored the whole of the human condition, explored the mastery of the unconscious, explored how people acted without the trappings of society or interaction with other people to define themselves.

To Dez, it sounded like a story almost completely without dialogue. To be treated like the experimental meanderings of David Foster Wallace—*The Broom of the System*, perhaps, or even Hemingway's turd of a novel *Across the River and Into the Trees*. To the untrained observer—one who hadn't been the beneficiary of a LexisNexis search—*The Apex and the Mountain Lion* might sound like a bold experiment, a rock star recording a classical album, a painter making a sculpture, but to Dez, she saw it for what it was: the last gasp of a thief, a hack, a liar, trying to prove he still had something that he had never had.

And so Dez listened to Frank Bethany's first chapter, about a white man setting out in the Argentine wilderness to ascend Mount Aconcagua, one of the tallest peaks in the world. It wasn't a mountain Dez had heard of before.

After Bethany's reading of his opening chapter, he began to talk about the history of the summit, the German explorer who first tried it, and the British mountaineer who succeeded about fifteen years after the first attempt. "But," he said, "Aconcagua isn't considered a difficult climb."

"I've read that too," Rebecca Foster said. "I heard that the northern route doesn't even require ropes or pins or anything like that."

"Still," Bethany said, "the year I climbed it, five climbers died. They underestimate the effects of cold weather, of the high altitude, and of the thin air."

A half-smile came over Dez's face. She thought about Frankie deciding to take Bethany on—and Bethany's publishing company. Frankie saw a well-worn path to proving her intellectual property, but was unprepared for the high altitude of the publishing company's lawyers and the cold temperatures of her boyfriend abandoning her. She half-wondered if Frankie had perhaps ascended Aconcagua first and had *that* story stolen from her as well. Or perhaps it was another female student enamored of both mountain climbing and Frank Bethany.

Her mind wandered, and she snapped back to the present when Rebecca Foster said, "...and of course, your most popular book to date, your debut novel, *Exodus Nights*."

Bethany smiled broadly to another wave of applause that broke out. "You know, I never thought when I was writing that manuscript that I would never live it down," he said.

"Live it down?" Rebecca Foster asked.

"Well, of course," Frank Bethany said. "It's not like any artist wants to be best-known for the first thing he puts out into the world. Imagine if the Beatles were only known for 'She Loves You' and not for 'Sergeant Pepper's.'"

Rebecca Foster laughed, and it took a split second for Frank Bethany to join her in her laughter.

"But of course I'll answer questions," Bethany said.

"There's just so much bravery in the book," Rebecca Foster said. "I don't think I've ever seen a scene with the people, um, having sexual relations, who turn into wolves and then insects."

"It was a particularly vivid dream that I had," Frank Bethany said, flatly, as though he were reciting it from memory at an elementary school play rehearsal. He then went through the details of the dream, discussing a particularly explicit lovemaking bout with his then-wife, making sure to make it sound like he was an excellent, well-endowed lover.

Dez had heard people like Frank Bethany wax poetic about their abilities before, expanding their accomplishments into areas where they hadn't gone, pushing out the other people who had helped along the way. The longer Frank Bethany talked, the more she felt sorry for Frankie, and then the pity turned into a righteous anger; that Frankie was justified in trying to take his identity, even if she had just done it for a cute girl she was trying to impress.

But as pity and righteous anger warred in her brain, there was thunderous applause and she saw Frank Bethany standing up and bowing again—center, stage left, stage right—and she realized the performance—or whatever this was—was over.

"We're not finished with our conversation," Audrey said. Dez realized that she was still holding Audrey's hand. She was hoping she hadn't been squeezing it too tight when she was thinking about how righteously angry she was.

"I really did enjoy that," Dez said.

"I barely even knew who this guy was before I met you," Audrey said. "I started reading him because of you. He's really talented. I love the way he writes."

Dez looked at Audrey. "Even his new book?"

Audrey looked unsure of herself for a second, and then set her jaw. "From the passages he just read? Yes, *especially* his new book. I like those man-versus-nature stories. I used to love animal stories when I was little. *Haunt Fox, Big Red*—all the Jim Kjelgaard books. I used to close my eyes and pretend I was a fox running wild in the snow."

Dez shrugged and nodded. "Okay," she conceded. "It's a pretty big departure from *Exodus Nights*, but I can see how you'd like it if you like those types of novels."

"*Those* types of novels?"

"Now, come on, Audrey, don't be like that. You know what I mean."

"After telling me that you slept with Jennifer Morgenstern, no, I'm not really sure what you mean."

Dez was quiet for a moment. "I probably should have told you earlier."

"You picked the shittiest possible time to tell me." Audrey stood up. "But I'm not going to let that stop me from buying his new book and getting him to sign it. You coming with me?"

Dez really didn't want to, but knew that getting their books signed was something Audrey considered more impressive than the tickets themselves. "Sure," Dez said, smiling. "I'll get mine signed too. I kind of wish I had a hardcover with me—I'll feel a little silly with the paperback."

"We've been over this, Dez," Audrey said, coldly, and then turning, she threaded her way through the crowd and into the large lobby area, where a line was quickly forming in front of a large table. They got in line, with about a hundred and fifty people in front of them.

They stood next to each other in an uncomfortable silence. Minutes ticked by, and the line crawled.

Dez saw a cashier's desk near the front and nudged Audrey. "I think you have to buy the book first before you get him to sign it."

Audrey looked up and saw a short line in front of the cashier's desk. People walked away with hardbacks of the new book. "Stay here."

Dez watched her as she got out of line and went to the cashier's desk. Audrey looked great in the dress, and Dez had found herself enjoying being dressed up with her. She kicked herself for bringing up her one-night stand with Frankie.

Audrey walked back with *The Apex and the Mountain Lion* tucked under her arm. Her face had softened and her jaw looked more relaxed.

"I'm really sorry," said Dez.

Audrey sighed. "It's not that I mind that you slept with someone before me. It's that I've been killing myself to find this book for you, and—well, I wouldn't have gone through all that trouble if I knew it was your ex."

"Not even an ex. We went on *one* date."

Audrey looked at Dez sideways. "But you slept with her—how long before me? Was it even a week?"

Dez was quiet.

"It's just—I feel like a fool," Audrey said, and her voice caught.

"You and I? We have something special," Dez said, disliking the note of desperation that crept into her voice. "I really like you, Audrey. And I didn't bring it up to you because, well, it didn't seem to matter. Not after the first night I spent with you."

Audrey shook her head, as if trying to clear her mind. "Fine," she said.

The line continued to move slowly, and they both started to get restless. When they were about five people from the front of the line, Dez looked at her watch. They had been waiting for a little over an hour. A deeply tanned white woman with big, feathered blonde hair about ten years out of style was talking Frank Bethany's ear off. He was smiling and nodding as best he could to try to close down the conversation and hurry her along, but she was having none of it, blocking the people behind her. Dez noticed that she hadn't purchased a book but had several dog-eared Frank Bethany novels with her. Dez thought idly that perhaps she had purchased them all at a used bookstore for fifty cents each and was trying desperately to inflate her self-importance. She may have had designs on going back to the same used bookstore to sell the signed copies for a profit.

Dez shook her head; sometimes her imagination ran away with her. Her hand was starting to cramp from carrying both *Exodus Nights* and *Murder on a Lifeboat*.

The woman finally walked away, and, as if in apology, the next four people in line simply got their books signed, murmured what big fans they were, and ducked their heads like they were embarrassed to have seen the big-haired woman's spectacle. Frank Bethany looked up at the line and raked his gaze over Dez before meeting her eyes.

"You're next," he said.

"My friend just bought your new book," she said, and Audrey set down her copy of *The Apex and the Mountain Lion* in front of him.

"Who should I make it out to?" he asked, smiling the same fake smile he had worn on stage.

"Audrey," Dez responded, nudging her. Audrey crossed her arms.

"Have him sign your copy of *Exodus Nights* too," Audrey said.

"I don't know—" Dez began.

"Sorry," Audrey said. "My friend Desirée is apparently embarrassed that she has one of your paperbacks instead of a hardback. But I told her you'd *gladly* sign it."

"Of course," he said.

Dez rolled her eyes and set the paperback of *Exodus Nights* down in front of him, next to *The Apex and the Mountain Lion*.

Frank Bethany's eyes went to the cover of *Murder on a Lifeboat*. "What the hell is that?" he said in a whisper.

Dez realized the problem—she wasn't sure what she had expected, though. Actually, she *did* realize what she had expected. She had expected Frank Bethany not to recognize the book he stole from. Or, she thought, maybe part of her still didn't even believe Frankie enough to even consider the possibility that Frank Bethany would freak out about it.

"I don't know what you're playing at," Frank Bethany hissed, "but get the hell out of line. And don't *ever* come to one of my events again."

Dez was so shocked she didn't move for a few seconds, but as the security guard began to step forward, she found her voice and her feet. "Sorry," she mumbled. "I didn't realize it would upset you." She tugged on Audrey's arm. "Come on, let's go."

"What's happening?" Audrey said.

"He saw the other book."

And then behind Audrey, another female voice released a bloodcurdling scream.

12

FRANKIE.

Dez pulled Audrey behind her; Audrey caught her heel on the carpet and fell to the floor.

Dressed in black jeans and a black hooded sweatshirt, Frankie came screaming into Dez's view. She knocked over the display of *The Apex and the Mountain Lion* and something glinted in her right hand.

A hunting knife.

Frank Bethany jumped out of his chair but couldn't move out of the way fast enough, and Frankie slashed out with the blade. It caught Bethany's right forearm, cutting through the sleeve of the tweed jacket. A small spray of blood came out as Bethany stumbled backward.

Frankie was screaming, but Dez couldn't make out what she was saying. Frankie raised the knife again.

Bang. Bang. Bang.

Dez saw Frankie's body contort and twist in midair, the knife held out awkwardly in front of her. Her head snapped back once, then twice, and a spray of red came out of her temple and a larger spray from her neck. Dez saw, out of focus, as if she were looking at the background of a photograph, the security guard, a large, silver .45 in his hand, smoke curling lazily out of the barrel.

"Frankie!" Dez wanted to shout, wanted to scream, but there was chaos. A man behind her pushed her down, on top of Audrey. She saw nothing but feet and legs, the sounds of panicked yelling, people telling each other to get out. The table was overturned. Dez covered Audrey, only vaguely aware that her girlfriend was screaming.

She turned, trying to go onto her back, and from the corner of her eye, she saw a door into the auditorium close. Did the security officer whisk Frank Bethany in there and close the door behind them?

She looked back down at Audrey, who was crying.

"Are you okay?"

"I don't know," she responded. "Are we dead?"

"No," Dez said. "Are you hurt?"

"I think I hurt my arm when I fell," Audrey said. "And I don't know where my purse is."

Dez slowly got up and caught her breath. She walked over to the overturned table and looked behind it. Frankie—also known as Jennifer Morgenstern—was lying behind it, her body warped into an odd, nauseating pose, and she was missing most of the left side of her face. Blood was pooling on the carpeted floor. Dez had dropped *Murder on a Lifeboat* and it had landed underneath Frankie's outstretched elbow.

Dez didn't see where her copy of *Exodus Nights* had gone, but she did see Audrey's purse. She bent down and picked it up. She turned back to Audrey, who was still lying on the floor.

Audrey's arm was bleeding.

"Oh, shit," Dez said.

"I don't—" Audrey began, and then started to cry again.

Dez pulled the tablecloth free from the overturned table, then dove down and pressed the tablecloth over the wound in Audrey's arm.

"Call 911!" she shouted. "Get an ambulance! She's been hit!"

There was more commotion as people started shouting. Dez kept the pressure on the wound; it wasn't as bad as it could have been. It looked like it missed the bone, and there wasn't enough blood for it to have hit an artery.

"My dress is ruined," Audrey said quietly.

"You're going to be okay," Dez said. "We're going to get you to a hospital and you're going to be okay."

"No, I'm not," Audrey said. "I'm not going to be okay ever again."

"Don't say that," Dez said into her ear. "I care about you too much. Please. We'll get through this."

"Who was that woman?" Audrey said.

Dez felt her heart sink. She swallowed. She thought she could hear sirens. "That was Jennifer Morgenstern."

Audrey looked at her in the eyes. They were a little unfocused. "Jennifer Morgenstern? The one who wrote that book I bought you? The one you slept with?"

Dez swallowed hard.

Audrey closed her eyes. "Am I dreaming this?"

"Let's just get you to the hospital," Dez said, and the tablecloth was now soaked with blood where Dez was holding it with her right hand over her wound. Audrey started to shake, but whether it was because she was losing blood, or scared out of her mind, or emotionally overwhelmed, Dez didn't know.

"I've never been shot before," Audrey said as the doors opened and two paramedics rushed in.

"Me neither," Dez said. The paramedics took over and Dez stood up and stepped back. She felt wetness on her face and wiped it off with her left hand. She expected it to be blood. She was surprised to see that her hand came away damp with tears.

———◆———

The paramedics told Dez that she wasn't allowed to ride in the ambulance before she even asked. After the ambulance drove off, a white, mustachioed police officer came up to Dez.

"I understand you were in the front of the line," he said. "Are you okay to answer a few questions?

Dez nodded. She answered his questions. He smiled when she told him she was getting her criminal justice degree.

Yes, she and her friend were there for the Frank Bethany reading. No, she hadn't seen the woman with the knife in the theater during the performance.

"The woman who was killed was Jennifer Morgenstern," Dez offered.

The officer's eyebrows raised. "How do you know her name? Do you know her?"

Dez thought about the dress with the red cherries, the point of the cheesecake, the East German woman and the silver-tipped arrow, the murder on the lifeboat, waving goodbye to the silhouette of Frankie.

"I know her book," Dez said. "She thought Frank Bethany plagiarized it."

The officer nodded. "Interesting. Do you know if she threatened him before today?"

Dez shrugged. "I know she sued him a few years ago and lost."

When the officer was finished asking her questions, she walked out into the pouring rain and drove Audrey's car to the Kaiser hospital off the Santa Monica freeway.

She stayed in the waiting room for two hours, anxious. She thought about what she might have done differently. Should she have called Frankie back? Should she have told Audrey about the night she spent with Frankie earlier? When she figured out that Frankie had really gotten her book stolen, should she have reached out to her then?

But Dez didn't know what she would have said in any of those situations. If she had returned Frankie's call, she would have only told Frankie that she had started seeing someone else. If she had had a conversation with Audrey about Frankie, it would have been as stilted and difficult as this one had been—or it might have been to cancel that book order. If she had reached out to Frankie about the stolen book—well, she wouldn't have known what to say; Frankie didn't even know that Dez knew her real name.

She looked at her watch: 11:59 P.M.

"Happy birthday to me," Dez said quietly.

A few minutes later, Audrey appeared, her upper arm wrapped in a bandage, accompanied by a nurse. "About twenty stitches," the nurse said, too cheerfully for the middle of the night. "Her vitals look strong. She didn't lose that much blood, considering. Missed the artery."

"You were lucky," Dez said, and felt the relief wash over her.

"They're letting me go home," Audrey said.

Dez drove. Audrey curled up into a ball on the passenger seat on the way back to her apartment. Dez explained everything to her—the conversation she had originally had with Frankie, when Frankie had taken credit for Frank Bethany's work, the research Dez had done in the library that helped convince her that Frank Bethany had plagiarized the book.

"How many times did you sleep with her?" Audrey said.

"With Frankie?"

"Or Jennifer, or whoever she was."

"It was just once," Dez said. "I know, I know, it was right before you and I started dating. But it was also before I realized she was lying to me about who she was."

They walked together to the stairs that went up to Audrey's apartment; the rain was finally starting to dissipate, and Dez was hoping the long rainy season would be over soon. Audrey nodded many times when Dez was telling her about everything, but didn't ask any questions.

Dez had plenty of questions, still. Who was Aaron? How had the publishing company gotten the suit dropped? But she didn't have any of the answers, and so didn't even mention the questions. She didn't want Audrey to think this would continue; she wanted to be done with Frankie and *Murder on a Lifeboat* and Frank Bethany. When Dez was finally all talked out, she gave Audrey a sad but hopeful smile that Audrey didn't return.

"I'm really tired," Audrey said. "I need to get some sleep." Something in her tone made it clear that Dez wasn't going to be staying the night.

"Sure," said Dez.

Dez didn't have her car, but didn't want to push it—she had put Audrey through enough for one night. Saying goodnight, Dez wanted to wrap Audrey in her arms and kiss her on the mouth, but Audrey just turned and walked up the stairs to her apartment.

As Dez walked to Pine Street, the rain completely stopped. A couple of cabs passed; Dez tried to flag down the first one without success, but the second one stopped for her.

When she arrived at her apartment, she saw lights on in the living room; she made sure to make a lot of noise when opening the front door, and by the time she finally stepped inside, she saw two pairs of feet padding upstairs toward Rhonda's room.

The next day, Audrey didn't call, and Dez and Rhonda had their first roommate-bonding night in a couple of weeks. They went to get burgers at a place near the ocean, and got their orders to go so they could sit on the beach and people-watch as the sun dipped down beneath the horizon. Dez, unprompted, told Rhonda what had happened.

Rhonda was enraptured by the story—a little too enraptured, as she didn't even tell Dez about the girl who had stayed over the night before. She asked questions in all the right places, and tut-tutted and gasped and swore appropriately.

"But Audrey is really freaked out," Dez said.

"She should be, though, right?" Rhonda asked. "I mean, you've got a hot ass and all, but you sure ain't worth getting shot."

"Yeah," Dez agreed, glumly.

"Don't you want to know what happened?" Rhonda said. "Don't you want to, I don't know, get a ticket to New Hampshire and find out who Aaron is, and why he abandoned Frankie, and whether or not Frankie had some kind of psychotic break? Don't you want to tell everyone that Frank Bethany is a fraud? That *Exodus Nights* is just blatantly stolen?"

"Not really," said Dez, hugging her knees. "I just want to go back to the aquarium with Audrey."

EPILOGUE

THE REST OF THE SPRING BREAK WEEK PASSED, AND Audrey didn't call, and no one picked up when Dez called.

She read the initial news articles about Morgenstern and Bethany, small articles that didn't mention the plagiarism suit. Dez read Jennifer Morgenstern's obituary in *The Los Angeles Times*, which was more delicate than it could have been. She also talked over the incident with Dr. Gallows, who was fascinated that Dez had gotten so close to a shootout, but he tried to show more concern than excitement. Dez told him she was in line when it happened, but didn't let him know that she was at the front of the line when Jennifer Morgenstern was shot right in front of her. She wanted more advice about the book and the plagiarism. He shrugged and said he doubted there was anything that could be done, especially when the author in question was deceased. Dez was trying to figure out what she felt about Frankie, but when she looked at her emotions it was just a mass of confusion and numbness.

But James Morgenstern, Jennifer's father, was not so confused or so numb. He flew to Los Angeles to give interviews to anyone who would listen about the book found under Morgenstern's elbow. He read passages on the radio of both *Murder on a Lifeboat* and *Exodus Nights*. He talked about how Jennifer's publishing house had tricked her into signing away her rights. He named Bethany's agent and a vice president at the publishing house and used the word "predatory." And he announced a lawsuit on behalf of his daughter's estate. The shooting and the lawsuit dominated the news for a few days, and then went quiet.

Dez considered going to the bookshop to talk to Audrey, but it was so out of her way she knew she'd look desperate. Dez moped around the apartment, although sometimes Rhonda, when she wasn't entertaining guests, could convince Dez to go to dinner or a movie.

Dez started applying for positions in the area, and secured interviews at a couple of police precincts. The sheriff's department from Estancia, the little town on the Central Coast where Audrey and Dez had gone on their weekend away, wanted her to drive up for an interview, and she left after Dr. Gallows's class the following Friday. She loved the drive up there, and the sheriff talked about sponsoring Dez through a certification program. Before she left, she drove by the hotel where she and Audrey had stayed, but it made her too sad to stop.

One Thursday afternoon when class was cancelled, Dez drove to BookEarth on Artesia Boulevard, only to find that Audrey had quit to work at a museum, although the older woman behind the counter didn't remember which one.

Rhonda finally persuaded Dez to go out dancing with her on Memorial Day Weekend and they met another pair of roommates, Shauna and Elyse, when they were dancing. Rhonda and Elyse were making out on the dance floor before Dez had even bought Shauna a drink. Dez drove everyone back to their apartment, and Elyse was in Rhonda's bedroom less than five minutes after they arrived. Dez and Shauna stared at the midnight movie on the USA Network, Dez desperately wanting to call Audrey. Shauna fell asleep on the couch before the movie was over. Dez made everyone breakfast in the morning.

Both Rhonda and Dez graduated on June twelfth. Dez's mother finally braved the airplane trip from Lake Charles to see her graduate. Rhonda's parents drove down from the Central Valley, but her father wouldn't look Rhonda in the eyes.

The Estancia sheriff's department left a message on their answering machine, which Dez heard when they returned from their graduation dinner. The department officially offered to sponsor her for certification training, and said they would offer her a job upon successful completion of the program. She called back the next day and accepted.

Dez had been on the job for three weeks, when, after work one day, she put a name into the new computer system—*Aaron Hawthorne*. Of the three hits she got in southern New Hampshire, only one was the right age. That Aaron Hawthorne had died of a heroin overdose in 1989. Dez was surprised by the bubble of rage she felt—why had he skipped out on Jennifer Morgenstern? Had he been bribed? Had he been high? Had he reconsidered? The dead end was staring Dez in the face, and the realization hit her in the pit of her stomach—she'd never know the answers. It made her nauseated.

The next week, she saw in the *Estancia Courier* that the estate of Jennifer Morgenstern settled for an undisclosed sum with Frank Bethany and Showcase Monument Publishing. The vice president whom James Morgenstern had accused left the company "to pursue other opportunities." James Morgenstern was quoted as saying that the result wouldn't bring Jennifer back, but he hoped the lawsuit would prevent other young authors from going through the same thing.

The following February, after getting off work, Dez got a package in the mail. She opened it up—a copy of *Murder on a Lifeboat*.

She opened the front cover and a note fell out.

Dez,

I'm sorry for never calling you back, and for never picking up the phone. By the time I was ready to get you back into my life, you had left for Estancia. It took me a while to track you down.

I wish things between us had gone differently, and I know it's too late to reconcile anything. But know that being with you was the best three months of my life.

Don't ask me what I had to do to get another copy of this damn book. Just know that this is a symbol of what we had for those brief weeks. Sometimes I feel like all we did was try to get out of the rain.

I hope you find what you're looking for.

Love,

Audrey

OTHER RELEASES

I'd love to hear what you thought of *Bad Weather*. Please leave reviews on Goodreads, BookBub, and your favorite online bookstore site.

Want more Dez Roubideaux?

Dez stays in Estancia, and twenty-five years later, is working as a detective sergeant in the county coroner's office when she meets new coroner Fenway Stevenson. The **Fenway Stevenson Mysteries** are available wherever books are sold:

The Reluctant Coroner: *www.books2read.com/Fenway1*
The Incumbent Coroner: *www.books2read.com/Fenway2*
The Candidate Coroner: *coming soon*

I'm hard at work on more Fenway Stevenson Mysteries—with Dez joining Fenway to solve murders and shut down conspiracies!

Join my mailing list—I write reviews of other mystery books, send info about free and discount mysteries and thrillers, and of course, you can be the first to know about my new releases: title and cover reveals, links to special videos, and more!

Visit *www.paulaustinardoin.com* to join my mailing list!